Thank You, Theo

Premila James

TWO OCEANS PUBLISHING

2015

**TWO OCEANS
PUBLISHING**

Published by Two Oceans Publishing

PO Box 1718
West Perth
WA 6872
Australia

ISBN 978-0-9943172-1-6

www.TwoOceansPublishing.com.au

Chapter 1

The Family Thorne

Have you ever been called a weirdo?

I have. Can you believe it? At school today Wayne Galbraith called me a weirdo.

Just like that.

A weirdo.

As you can probably guess I didn't like it. No, I have to say that I didn't like it one little bit. It's the first time I've ever been called anything like that and I really don't know why he did it.

Wayne Galbraith should not have called me a weirdo. As far as I can see he had no real reason to do so. In fact, here are three very good reasons why he should *not* have called me a weirdo:

1. Wayne Galbraith knows nothing about me.

2. It isn't nice calling people weird (even if they are a bit odd).

3. I am not a weirdo.

I've been thinking about it a lot and I'm still not sure why Wayne Galbraith did this to me. I mean, I don't think that I look weird or act weird, and I've never done anything to him. Well, not that I can think of, anyway. I don't think that I have even spoken to him all that often. Yet he still called me a weirdo.

If anything, I reckon that Wayne Galbraith is weirder that I could ever possibly be. In fact, there are several kids in my class who, in my opinion, are far more deserving of the tag "weirdo" than I am. So why did he say it to me? As you can imagine, his comment has really been niggling at me.

Here's how it happened.

It was a Friday afternoon and because it was a Friday everyone was in a good mood. We had just finished up for the day and for most of us our attention had already turned to the weekend. The siren had gone and through the windows we could see kids spilling out from other classes and streaming towards the school gates.

As always on a Friday afternoon our teacher, Mr Cranston, jumped to his feet as soon as the school siren went off. He shouted his usual "School's out; bye bye nerds," and then bolted for the exit.

He was fond of Fridays, was our Mr Cranston. From the way he charged across the room with his knees up high and his fists pumping a casual observer might think that he didn't like being at school. We knew better though . . . I think.

Anyway, that afternoon poor Ellen Alford was a little slow getting out of the way and Mr Cranston knocked her off her crutches in his haste to get to the door. Pretending not to notice, he wrenched the door open and tore through it like a man with his hair on fire.

All in all, it was pretty much a normal kind of Friday afternoon departure for Mr Cranston. If it wasn't Ellen getting knocked over then it was bound to be one of the other pupils. I too had been flattened on a couple of occasions, but after my most recent experience I had taken to holding back from the door on a Friday afternoon, at least until after Mr Cranston had gone.

Poor Ellen wasn't so lucky. Not only was she hampered by having a leg in plaster, but her desk was situated pretty well directly between Mr Cranston's desk and the door. She had been returning to her desk from the front of the class when the siren went off. Panicked, she froze like a baby deer caught in headlights and that was her undoing. Mr Cranston went through her like a truck through a fence made of spaghetti.

One of the girls helped Ellen to her feet and another picked up the paper and pens that the force of the collision had left scattered all over the floor. The rest of us packed up and put away our possessions and starting leaving at a more dignified pace.

I was in no particular hurry and I usually took my time gathering my things and neatly arranging my desk. As a result I was always one of the last through the door. I had just come out of the classroom and was zipping up my bag and putting my empty water bottle into its little pouch when Wayne Galbraith struck. He walked over to me, dragging his bag behind him.

Wayne Galbraith is a big, untidy kid with green eyes and red hair. Well, he's big compared to me, I suppose. I'm probably about average size for a twelve year old.

Outside of class Wayne will often be found sucking on a lollipop. If he's not sucking on a lollipop then it is likely that he will be chewing on the end of a used lollipop stick or rolling a used lollipop stick from one corner of his mouth to the other. I expect he thinks it looks cool to roll a used lollipop stick around his mouth but to me it just looks idiotic.

As Wayne shambled messily in my direction he reminded me of an orangutan dragging a branch or a dead gibbon along the ground. Take off his school uniform and throw a bit of orange hair onto his body and the two would be indistinguishable. Well, that's my opinion, anyway. I expect Wayne's mother and father might have thought differently.

In case you're wondering, and I expect that you probably are, I know a fair bit about orangutans and other primates. I had just finished a very detailed and entertaining science project on them. So I'm packed with primate information. I could almost be one, I know so much about them.

Here are some facts for you. Did you know that the pygmy marmoset is the world's smallest monkey? One could sit on the palm of your hand quite easily. You might not want it to, though, just in case it had rabies or it decided to do a poo there.

Or did you know that human birth control pills also work on gorillas? I bet you didn't know that one.

Now here's something strange to think about. Did you know that some scientists once gave a number of baby chimpanzees a load of different toys to play with and the boy chimpanzees went straight for the cars and trucks and the girl chimpanzees went straight for the dolls?

It's true; I'm not making any of this up. It's interesting, isn't it?

As I said, I know a lot of cool stuff about primates. If you need to know what the silky sifaka prefers to eat or you'd like to know the correct name for the giant ape that's attacking you and trying to rip your head off then come and see me. I'll set you right. I'm almost an expert.

Anyway, back to the orangutan heading in my direction.

Most of our classmates had already left for the day and were either going home or were heading across to the oval for the week's final kick-around. Wayne and I were really the only people left in that part of the playground.

Wayne was by himself so I couldn't even say that he was being egged on by his friends or was trying to show off. Which might have made what he did next a bit more understandable. After all, kids are always doing stupid things to try to impress the people around them. But no, it was just the two of us and a school classroom is a lonely place when there are no other people around.

Now brace yourself, my friend, because here it comes. What a way to end the school week.

"You're a weirdo," Wayne said, putting his big face right up close to mine. On his breath I could smell the ham sandwich he had eaten for lunch. And the strawberry milk he had washed it down with.

Gross.

I mean, there's no other possible description for it. It was *gross*. As one would expect when someone like that puts his mouth close to your face and breathes all over you. No surprise there.

His words, though, *had* taken me by surprise, I have to

admit it. I was stunned and I didn't know how to respond. So I just took a step back from him and waited for him to say something else.

He stared at me with those blank green eyes. The only bit of intelligence I could see in them was my own reflection. Then he opened his scungy mouth and I could see his grotty teeth and right down his vile pink throat past the little dangly bit.

Not a pretty sight.

I kept waiting. No more words came. After a moment Wayne burped loudly in my face and laughed. Then he turned and walked away.

Gross.

Double gross.

In fact, it's more than double gross, it's double disgusting. Double disgusting with a side serve of revolting.

For a moment I couldn't move and I certainly couldn't breathe. So I just stood there trying to exhale continuously for minutes on end and watched him go. He swung his bag over his shoulder and shuffled off, grunting and giggling to himself.

Off in the distance I could see Wayne Galbraith's mother waiting for him on the other side of the school gate. She looked at me and smiled, and then gave a little wave. She was some distance away and I was in shock, so I pretended not to notice her and picked up my own backpack.

By that time I had emptied my lungs and could exhale no further without passing out or keeling over or something similar. My heart was racing and I felt as though my chest was about to collapse in on itself.

I took a giant breath. Fresh clean air, finally. Pure air. I took another breath and then another. I could feel my heart start to slow.

Wayne was by now half way to the gate and I was standing alone outside my classroom. Thank goodness for that. Peace and solitude at last.

Mrs Galbraith, who was friends with my mother, gave another wave. Despite the filthy outrage her son had just committed on me I could not stop myself from giving her a little wave back.

Mrs Galbraith was nice and friendly, but the same could not be said for the abomination she had mothered. What was he doing, burping into my face like that? Not to mention calling me names. No one had ever called me a name like that before.

Well, maybe they had, but not so blatantly, not directly to my face. Surely Wayne knew that it wasn't nice to call people names. Frankly, it was more than not nice, it was unacceptable. It simply wasn't on. But it had happened.

I decided there and then that if Wayne Galbraith went around calling people names then he must be some kind of numbskull. And a knucklehead to boot. Not to mention a lamebrain of the highest order. Or should that be the lowest order?

Whatever.

I'm sure you get the picture.

Some people – like the bullies and name-callers of this world – are real idiots and cannot help themselves. As far as I was concerned Wayne Galbraith had just joined that club as a life-member.

As I slowly made my way to the school gate I kept

wondering why Wayne Galbraith had approached me and why he had called me a weirdo.

Perhaps it's because I write with my left hand and eat my sandwiches with my right hand. Perhaps it's because I don't like sport. Perhaps it's because I like drawing and writing stories and all he ever does is throw rocks, suck on lollipops and play football.

Once I heard the deputy principal ask Wayne Galbraith whether he would prefer to be the smartest kid in the class or the fastest. I'm sure you can guess what he said.

The fastest, of course. What else would you expect from someone like that? And he calls me a weirdo!

Now let's just pause here for a moment. Here I am, telling you all about me and my problems at school and I don't know the first thing about you. Well, here's an opportunity for me. Why don't I put the same question to you? Your answer will help me to understand the kind of person you are.

Here it is, then. What would you rather be, the smartest kid in your class or the fastest?

Before you answer, be careful of what you say. If you say that you'd rather be the smartest kid in your class then people like Wayne Galbraith will think that you're a weirdo. If you say that you'd rather be the fastest kid in your class then people like me will think that you're a weirdo (although we'd probably never say it to your face). So what's it going to be?

Smartest?

Fastest?

I expect that, like me, you're thinking how much you'd like to be both the smartest and the fastest kid in your class.

I know I'd like that. I think that I'd like that more than anything else in the world. But I know that I'm not the smartest kid in my class and I'm certainly not the fastest.

I'm sure that there might be a few people on this earth who could be both the fastest and smartest kid in their class. To be honest, though, I think that this situation would have to be exceptionally rare.

In every class you would have to have one kid who was the smartest and one kid who was the fastest. That stands to reason. In any group there will always be a smartest and a fastest. But I think that you would hardly ever find that the smartest and fastest would be the same kid. Nine hundred and ninety-nine times out of a thousand it would be two different kids. It has to be.

In fact, the great majority of kids in the world are neither the fastest in their class or the smartest in their class. Most kids are somewhere in the middle.

Anyway, even if you're the slowest kid in your class or the dumbest kid in your class it doesn't mean anything. All it means is that you're probably in a class full of really smart and really fast kids. Outside of that class there are bound to be loads of kids who are slower or dumber than you are.

So what's it to be, then? What would you rather be; the smartest kid in your class or the fastest?

Tricky, isn't it?

I think that it's tricky. My dad often says that life is an awfully twisted revolting mess and that it's full of tricky questions. That must be one of the tricky questions.

Anyway, to get back to Wayne Galbraith, I knew that I wasn't a weirdo. Despite what others – usually ignorant grown-ups – might have thought or said (but never to my face) I always considered myself quite boringly normal and not at all weird.

In fact, it is my firm belief that there are many people at school who are far weirder than I am. Take our teacher Mr Cranston, for instance. Now he is totally weird. If there's a book on weirdness then he wrote it. You couldn't get much weirder.

I would have to say that my good friends Leroy and Toby are also a lot weirder than I am. That goes without saying, even though I have just said it. Or written it, rather. And my best friend, Theodore Thorne, would have to be just about the weirdest person I know.

Not that I know that many people. Apart from my mum and dad I reckon I only really know about ten or eleven people. Of them, though, Theodore Thorne is easily the weirdest.

Definitely.

Although Leroy and Toby are not that far behind Theo, now that I think about it some more. Put them all together and you have three very weird dudes. Sometimes I wonder what I'm doing hanging out with them.

Weird.

All right, I suppose I should stop using the word weird. It's stuck in my head now, thanks to that knucklehead Galbraith.

Sorry about that.

So now I will try to rise above the level of people like Wayne Galbraith. I will simply say, instead of weird, that Theodore Thorne is the strangest and most interesting person that I know.

Definitely.

Theodore was the first person that I sat next to, and the first person who actually spoke to me, when I started at Hampton Primary a year ago.

Well, there were also some grown-ups and my teacher, I suppose, but they don't count. I'm talking about real people here.

Theodore was the first person who spoke to me that really mattered and after that he became my first friend at my new school and also my best friend.

I have a few more friends now but most of the other people in my class I don't really know very well. I mean, I know who they are and all that, but I don't know all that much about them.

Theodore, Leroy and Toby are the only ones I know a lot about. That's because they tend to hang around me a fair bit and I do the same with them.

It's probably a good thing that Theodore, Leroy and Toby spend a lot of time with me. It's good to have some friends, of course, and we often have a great time together. It's a lot of fun and it takes my mind off other things. I think that everyone needs some enjoyable distractions from time to time.

It's also a good thing that we are friends because Theodore wants me to keep a record of his life.

Yep, you read it correctly; Theodore wants me to keep a record of his life. He told me so. We had just finished a spelling test one day and he leaned over and whispered it to me. "I need you to keep a record of my life," he said in a confidential murmur. "Someone's going to have to and it might as well be you."

Which is why I started writing the book you are now

reading, flicking through or using to swat a mosquito. This book, about Theodore and my friendship with him, would probably have been a bit harder to write had Theodore and I not been friends. So it was just as well that we were.

Theodore is convinced that there are going to be some pretty amazing things happening around him before too long and he wants it all down on paper. It needs to be on the public record, he says. He can't, however, be bothered doing it himself. He's far too busy and important for that, he reckons, and anyway his handwriting is very messy. He's always getting told off about it at school.

You might think that Theodore is taking advantage of me by getting me to do this. This suits me, however, because my handwriting is neat and tidy and I quite like writing stories. I am also very good at spelling (I aced that test, in case you were wondering) and am pretty good at punctuation.

Also, I would rather tell you all about Theodore's life than my own life. You might find that hard to believe but it's true.

My life is pretty boring, to be honest, and there are some things in it that I would rather forget. So try to ignore me and focus all of your attention on Theodore. He loves being the centre of attention. You can spare a bit for Leroy and Toby, as well, as they are sometimes good for a laugh.

So here it is then.

The life story of Theodore Thorne, as observed by me and as written by me. An impartial account of his character, his habits, his behaviour and his misbehaviour.

Okay, so it may not be Theodore's life story, perhaps, as it only covers part of his final year of primary school. But it is a truthful record of a part of his life and it's an important part at that.

Well, as this book is about Theodore Thorne I suppose I should probably tell you something about him.

Theodore Thorne.

Theo for short.

Hmm. How should I begin?

Well, like me, Theo is twelve years old. But unlike me, Theo is an inventor and an explorer. I don't do any of that kind of stuff. Theo, on the other hand, just loves it.

Theo lives at home with his mother, father and sister. Theo's sister is called Filomena and she is two years older than him but at least ten times more annoying. Well, she's annoying to Theo, anyway. Other people seem to like her.

The Thorne family also has a dog named Winnie. He's a boy dog so everyone thinks his name is short for Winston. But it's not really. Filomena has always loved Winnie the Pooh and when their mother brought the puppy home he was round, fat and light brown. So they called him Winnie.

Theo's father said that Winnie was a good name for their new puppy. He held him high in the air and said in a booming voice, "Winnie the Pooh, eh? Well here's Winnie, all right, and there's poo everywhere."

I don't think Winnie was too happy about being lifted up like that. When Theo's father put him down on the floor again Winnie ran flat out three times around the room and then did a wee in Theo's empty school shoe.

In addition to Winnie the dog, Theo and Filomena have a cat named Tigger and four Siamese fighting fish. The fish need to be kept in separate tanks otherwise they will attack and try to eat each other.

Theo's father keeps threatening to get separate tanks for Theo and Filomena as well, and maybe one for his wife, too, although he doesn't say that when she's around.

Theo's father can put up with Winnie and the fish, and Theo and Filomena, but he's not too keen on Tigger. In fact, he didn't like Tigger very much at all. One day there had been an incident. It was an incident that should be in the book about his life, Theo said.

So here it is.

On the day of the incident, Theo told me, his father had come out of the shower drying his hair and he sat down heavily on his bed. With water still in his eyes he didn't see Tigger, who had started taking her afternoon naps there. Theo's father sat right on her.

Now that, as you can probably imagine, was a mistake. You can also probably imagine what happened next.

Apparently it was hard to determine which of the two, Theo's father or the cat, howled loudest. But after Tigger had raced off the bed and down the stairs like a furry grey bullet it was Theo's father who kept making all of the noise. He lay on the carpeted floor of his bedroom screaming and roaring and clutching his bleeding rump with both hands.

"I'm blind ... O mercy ... I'm blind!"

The rest of the household were immediately sent into a panic by the commotion. When all of the crashing and screaming started Theo's mother raced upstairs at full pelt to see what was going on. Unfortunately for Theo's father his wife had been having a coffee with their neighbour, Mrs Cartwright, at the time.

Mrs Cartwright is a well-built woman who works part-time at the nearby shopping mall as a retail security guard.

She is sturdy and athletic and has been on a ju-jitsu training course. She thundered up the stairs as well, getting her meaty fists into the ready position just in case she had to take on a burglar or two.

Apparently it didn't take too long for Theo's mother and Mrs Cartwright to assess the situation. It was pretty clear what had happened. Theo's father had sat squarely on the sleeping cat.

Pinned to the bedspread and momentarily defenceless against the offensive backside, Tigger somehow rolled, or squirmed, onto her back. Then she raked the naked rump with all four of her claws and took off.

Theo's father screamed and shot straight up into the air. As he descended the towel he had been drying his hair with wrapped around his face. His lacerated rear end landed on the edge of the bed and he screamed again and became airborne once more. His next and final destination was the floor, which he hit face first, leaving him dazed, in agony and very confused.

When Theo's mother and Mrs Cartwright burst like a tsunami into the room they were faced with Theo's father moaning and thrashing about on the floor with nothing but his fluffy blue towel wrapped tightly around his head. It was a pitiful sight.

On seeing Theo's father Mrs Cartwright sucked her breath in with horror, clapped her big hands over her eyes and peeked through the cracks in her fingers. It looked as though all her long-held misgivings about Theo's father were finally being confirmed.

Theo's mother, although equally horrified and repulsed by the sight, felt compelled to act. Like a caring and dutiful wife she knelt down beside her husband and took him in her arms. She gently lifted his head from the floor and rested it in her lap. Carefully she unwound the towel from around his head.

Then she slapped his face hard and yelled at him to snap out of it. Taking him by the shoulders, she followed her slap with a good shake and shouted at him for scaring the poor cat and getting blood on the bedspread.

Theo's father was still very confused and was suffering terrible pain. His eyes widened at this unexpected verbal and physical onslaught. Then when he saw Mrs Cartwright looming over his wife's shoulder his eyes looked as though they were about to pop out of his head. He squawked and started thrashing about wildly again. It looked as though he was having a fit. Perhaps he was trying to get up and out of there. Or get some clothes on, at least.

Mrs Cartwright, who had been secretly hoping for a sustained and bruising encounter with a big hairy intruder, could barely contain her disappointment. She looked at Theo's father and shook her head in disgust.

Hopeless, she appeared to be thinking. Hopeless and pathetic. After taking a final dismissive look she turned on her heel and walked out of the room.

When Theo and Filomena came running into the bedroom shortly after, their father's humiliation was complete. He gave up all hope of salvaging any shred of dignity from his position and slumped back onto the floor. He might even have cried a little bit.

His wife gave up and shoved him away with repugnance. Then she went off in search of poor Tigger, to make sure that she was all right. Theo and Filomena went with her.

"He's so embarrassing," Filomena kept saying to her mother as they made their way back down the stairs to the kitchen.

"Just so embarrassing. That's why I don't like having any of my friends over here when he's around. He's just so embarrassing …"

Those sorts of things seemed to happen a lot in the Thorne household. There always lots of drama and excitement going on. It was one of the reasons that I enjoyed going around there. It made my house and family appear positively boring. I guess I was lucky to be able to visit a house like that whenever I wanted to. It was never dull, I can tell you that.

Well, I can see that I have told you a little about Theo's family, and the animals that live in and around their house. But I really haven't said too much about Theo yet. I guess that now is probably a good time.

Chapter 2

Theodore Thorne - Inventor and Explorer

As I mentioned three or four pages ago, Theodore Thorne is an inventor and an explorer. He is mad about inventing stuff and exploration. It is probably true to say that the great passions in his life, apart from potato crisps and tomato sauce, are science and discovery. Theo lives and breathes these fields of endeavour.

Now, when I say inventing stuff I don't mean doing the sorts of things that you and I might do and call inventing. Like drawing a picture of a sports car with a cannon on the roof or making a robot out of plasticine that doubles as a toothbrush holder.

No, Theo does real inventing, using wires and tools and batteries and circuits and all sorts of complicated things. He actually builds things that have never been built before, and many of them even work. I'll tell you about some of his inventions a bit later.

When he is not at school, or asleep, Theo spends most of his time conducting scientific experiments, building things or undertaking all manner of dangerous and potentially deadly expeditions through the surrounding streets and countryside.

Well, he claims they are deadly; whether they are or not is another question. I'm not making any judgment on this; I'm just reporting the facts.

I suppose that getting out of bed in the morning could be potentially deadly if there happened to be a scorpion in one of your slippers or someone had spread butter on your floor and left a lot of big spikes lying about.

When Theo is not hard at work doing those sorts of things – experiments, building and exploration – he can usually be found reading about them or watching scientific or engineering documentaries. After all, he is a very curious and observant type of person. He knows loads about everything, is always on the search for new information and new ways of doing things, and his heroes are Newton and Copernicus.

No, Newton and Copernicus are not superstar Brazilian footballers. Well, I suppose they might be, but if so those dudes are not the ones we are talking about here. Get with the program, please. The sportsmen left through the side door some time ago. We are philosophers and scientists here.

Theo's Newton and Copernicus are not footballers; they are great men of science. I should say that they *were* great men of science. The two great men are both long dead. Theo did his science project on them.

Hang on a moment, those last two sentences sound a little bit funny together. Or maybe I am just being overly sensitive. Yes, it is true that the great scientists and mathematicians Isaac Newton and Nicolaus Copernicus are dead, long dead. And yes, Theo did do a science project on them recently. But that's not why they are dead – Theo had nothing to do with that. You can't pin that one on him.

Newton and Copernicus are dead because they lived hundreds of years ago.

I expect they died of old age. Or murder or drowning or germs or something. Whatever it was, I'm ninety-nine percent certain that Theo had nothing to do with it.

I don't think Theo mentioned how they died in his science project (there it is again – that sentence sounds funny as well). Maybe he should have, just to clear up any misunderstanding. Some people are awfully suspicious, after all.

For as long as he can remember Theo has had an insatiable curiosity and all of his spare time has been devoted to science and exploration. As a consequence he has always wanted to follow a similar path in life to the one that both his father and mother have taken.

But much better and more exciting, obviously.

After all, Theo's parents are both adults, and I don't think adults are capable of leading exciting lives. All of the adults I know are as boring as anything. All they seem to do is sit like dummies in front of the television or computer, or go to the supermarket or hardware store, or kneel in the garden weeping softly as they pull out weeds.

Theo's father and mother are scientists. Both are pretty good at what they do, apparently. Well, so Theo tells me, anyway.

Theo's father wears glasses and teaches geology at the nearby university, where he is also finishing off his doctoral studies in geophysics. He is very tall and lean. He is a keen environmentalist and on most days he rides an electric bicycle to and from work. He is also a science fiction buff.

Theo's mother wears contact lenses and tight dresses and is an engineer with a research institute in the city. She is also a keen environmentalist and drives a Porsche to work. She is interested in theatre, sculpture, the stock market and Greco-Roman wrestling.

Both of Theo's parents, if you haven't already guessed, are very smart. Filomena is smart, too, and she wears glasses as well. But she has contact lenses also, which she wears sometimes. Theo's father also has contact lenses but he never wears them.

Like his parents and sister Theo is also very smart and he also wears glasses. Theo hates contact lenses, though, and he thinks that glasses are much more dignified and practical.

Theo has modified his glasses, however, so that when he presses tiny buttons on the frame little aluminium screens fold down to cover each lens. He said they are designed to protect his eyes from hurricanes, fireballs, plagues of locusts and nuclear explosions. The glasses appear a little odd when the screens are up – Theo looks as though he has enormous silver eyebrows – but I thought they were a pretty cool invention.

Theo was pleased with them as well. "Your eyes are the most sensitive optical instrument you'll ever possess," he said. "They are very fragile and need to be protected at all times."

"So true," I replied, happy to agree with Theo's line of reasoning. Despite my initial interest and admiration, however, I was not completely convinced. "If you're in a fireball or a nuclear explosion, though, your eyes might be protected but won't the rest of you just get blown to bits?"

"Blown to bits, you say?"

"Yes."

"As in . . . ?"

"As in blown to bits. You know, blown to smithereens. Bits of you over here and bits of you over there. How else can I put it?"

Theo thought for a moment then took his glasses off and ran his fingers through his thin dark hair.

"I suppose that might happen," he said. "It probably depends on the situation. Perhaps I need to extend the shields so that when the need arises they can spread out further and cover the whole body."

"That should do it," I said. "Extendable shields."

"Yes," he agreed. "It might require a bit more work, that one. It could be a bit tricky, what with the weight and all. Thanks for the tip, and I'll look into it, but I think I'll keep them as they are for the moment."

"That's probably a good idea. No need to move too quickly."

"Correct."

"They are a great invention, though."

"Yes, they are, aren't they?"

"They're really good."

"Smashing."

Theo intends to be a brilliant inventor and an intrepid and successful explorer but he is not prepared to wait until he has finished school before he starts his work in these areas. He says that he has no time to lose. His career in science has already begun and with each day that passes his ideas get more inventive and elaborate. And it is my role, he insists, to stand at his side and document his work so that one day the world may read about him and learn of his triumphs.

Theo is very careful about who gets to see any of his projects, but as his best friend I have been granted access to most of them. Some, it must be said, are more successful than others. Despite my doubts, I had to consider his protective glasses a success.

Here is a small selection of some of Theo's other successful inventions:

1. The exploding mobile phone.

2. The automatic bicycle tyre deflator.

3. The exploding teddy bear.

4. The exploding packet of peanuts.

5. The portable alien detector.

Inventions 1 to 4 on the above list were designed to be operated remotely and they also incorporated a handy time-delay feature. Very useful for those of us who are not fast runners.

As you may have noticed, many of Theo's inventions tend to be explosive in nature. Now really, you shouldn't be too surprised by that. After all, what twelve-year-old doesn't like explosions? The last entry on the above list, though, doesn't have an explosive feature. Although given its nature perhaps it should. But it is an interesting invention. I'll tell you a bit about it now.

Our friend Leroy is fascinated by aliens and is convinced that one day the country will be invaded by swarms of them. This fascination started when Leroy was very young and over time it seems to have developed into a full-blown obsession. Now Leroy says he has difficulty sleeping as he is constantly thinking about the prospect, especially at bedtime. So when he's not in bed, and not at school, he spends much of his time searching the heavens for signs of alien spacecraft or training for that terrible day when the conflict between humans and aliens will begin.

Theo's parents believe that Leroy's obsession with aliens is unhealthy and that in the long term it will probably be detrimental to his health and well-being. Theo and I agreed with this assessment, so to help Leroy deal with this problem Theo invented the portable alien detector.

The portable alien detector is a very complicated and advanced piece of equipment and Theo spent about three weeks and more than forty dollars perfecting it. It is full of wires and old computer chips and is covered in an array of flashing lights and a rotating aerial. It now sits by the window in Leroy's bedroom, constantly scanning the neighbourhood for alien life.

Leroy was a little sceptical when Theo first presented the portable alien detector to him. Mind you, he wasn't the only one. Toby and I were dubious as well.

"Here," said Theo. "This is my new portable alien detector, or PAD. More specifically, it's the PAD-39. But don't worry, though, this one's not radioactive."

This was a reference to one of his earlier attempts at this kind of technology.

"Why have you called it the PAD-39?" asked Toby,

peering at the device and scowling. He poked it with a tentative finger.

"Why PAD-39? Why not the PAD-2 or PAD-5000 or something?"

"Well, if you really must know, it's been designated the PAD-39 because I worked my way through 39 jelly beans before I came up with the final design. Here Leroy, I'll lend it to you. Call it an early temporary birthday present. If an alien comes within five hundred metres of this little ripper it will light up like a Christmas tree and the alarm will go off."

"Really?" said Leroy, looking doubtful. He shouldered Toby aside and gave it a gentle prod with his finger.

"Really," said Theo.

"You're kidding me, right? This is a joke or something?"

"No, Leroy, I'm deadly serious."

Theo was often deadly serious. Probably about ten times a day, in fact.

"Does it really detect aliens?" Leroy didn't sound very convinced.

"Of course it does," said Theo. "I spent ages building this thing and it cost a packet. It's the only one in existence. Those pinheads at NASA tried building one and spent trillions on it. They fell flat on their faces though – their thing was a complete dud. The only time it went off was when the President walked by. Now this little beauty," Theo purred, rubbing his hands lovingly over his contraption, "This little beauty works like a dream. Make sure you look after it."

"But ... but ... how is it possible? How does it work?"

Leroy was starting to fidget and hop around now. He

was starting to get excited. With Leroy, this was not always a good thing.

Leroy was renowned for hopping around and fidgeting when he was excited and he once hopped into the back of a slowly reversing car when he saw a Lamborghini go tearing down the other side of the road.

Fortunately he wasn't hurt. A grazed knee, a bloody nose and a broken collarbone were all that he copped in that incident, although somehow the sole of one of his shoes was ripped clean off as well.

Now *that* was a mystery.

Try as we might, none of us who had witnessed the incredible event could explain how it happened. As Leroy picked himself up and tried to staunch the bleeding from his wounds with a tissue we all stood around and gazed in wonderment at the mangled remains of his school shoe. Even the postman who happened to be passing by at the time came over and stood with us for a while, shaking his head in bewilderment and fingering his heavy sack distractedly.

In the end we had no option but to add the incident to the *Catalogue of the Unexplained* that Toby was compiling in an old exercise book as one of life's great mysteries.

"How does the portable alien detector work, you ask?"

"Yes . . . yes."

"Well if you stop hopping about I'll tell you."

"Okay," said Leroy, "I've stopped."

"About time. That's a very annoying habit you have there. Now the PAD-39 really is quite simple," explained Theo. "It is extremely complicated, of course, but at the same time it's very simple."

"Okay, I think I'm with you."

"Good. You turn it on, like so, and if an alien comes into range the detector will detect it and sound a warning, like this."

Theo pressed a button on the base of the detector. The unit emitted a loud beeping noise and its lights started flashing. We all took a step back. With Theo's inventions an explosion was always a possibility. Theo shook his head in disgust. Then he removed his finger and the noise and lights stopped.

"You guys are hopeless. But that's all there is to it."

Theo passed the detector to Leroy. It had a black and grey casing and was about the size of a house brick.

"All right," said Leroy, warming to the idea. "Thanks. I'll take good care of it. I'll put it by the window here."

"Perfect."

"How do you set it up?"

"It's already on and calibrated. The batteries should last for months. Just leave it there and as long as it does nothing you'll know there are no aliens around."

"Really?"

"Really."

"Looks like you've done it again, Theo," said Toby.

"Yep."

"Well that's . . . brilliant," said Leroy, with a stunned expression on his face. He looked like he'd just been belted on the back of the head with a dead fish. "It's brilliant. This is top notch and it's just what I need. Thank you, Theo."

"No need for thanks, Leroy. Just look after it."

"I will, don't worry, I will."

"Excellent."

Many of Theo's inventions were similarly inspiring and worked just as he predicted. The portable alien detector, for instance, had been sitting by Leroy's window for the past eight months and was still working perfectly. In that whole time it had not flashed once nor emitted a single beep. As a result, Leroy was able to sleep in peace, comforted by the knowledge that there were no aliens in his garden or prowling around the neighbourhood preparing to attack the human race and take over the world.

Some of Theo's inventions, however, despite being imaginative and thought-provoking, were somewhat less successful. Here are a number of Theo's less successful inventions:

1. The cat flavoured dog biscuit.

2. The collapsible ladder.

3. The gas powered particle accelerator.

4. The gas powered hamster accelerator.

5. The hands-free toilet paper dispenser.

The last of those was a real failure, to be honest. A great idea, I'm the first to admit, but it was one that didn't really work too well in practice.

Okay, I can guess that some of you might be curious about what happened with that particular invention. So I'll tell you a little something about that one as well. Just to give you a bit more of an insight into Theo's complicated but interesting brain.

This invention was designed for people who couldn't be bothered wiping their bottom after using the toilet. Maybe they were too lazy, or they were eating a hamburger, or they were in the middle of a good part of a book and didn't want to stop reading.

I don't know.

There are probably a million reasons why you might not want to wipe your bottom after using the toilet but I'm not going to list them all here. You can do that yourself, if you really want to.

Anyway, Theo had convinced himself that this particular invention was one of those really useful ones which had the potential to revolutionize the world.

Now for some technical information.

Ordinarily I wouldn't bother including this sort of boring technical detail but this book is all about Theo and Theo wants the technical detail recorded.

To give the reader a better understanding of a brilliant mind.

Those are his words, not mine, which is why they are written like that.

So here it is.

The technical information.

You can skip it if you like.

The room containing the toilet required minimal modification; just a couple of small electrical engines with spooling mechanisms attached to the walls on each side of the toilet.

The idea is that when you have finished your business on the toilet you stand up and pivot ninety degrees either way. It doesn't matter which way. So if you sit on the toilet with your back to the cistern, like most boring people, after you get up and pivot you will be facing a side wall. This is the stance that is required for the invention to work properly.

Some people, however (myself among them), prefer to sit the other way around on the toilet. That is, straddling it and facing the cistern as though riding a motorcycle.

This is much more fun and allows you to make use of some of the sound effects that are often generated on those occasions. On some days you can pretend to be riding a huge motorcycle with a massive engine and a thunderous exhaust, while on others you can pretend to be on a little stuttering moped or some nearly silent electrical thing. Some days you don't know what you've got until you climb aboard. Other days it's like a jet-powered drag bike that starts with an explosion and throws flames out the rear.

Like I said, it can be great fun sitting this way, and when you get up and pivot you will also be facing a side wall.

Clever, isn't it?

I think it is.

If you sit on the toilet side-saddle or if your toilet is part of a larger bathroom with walls too far apart then you will have problems with this invention. A side-saddle sitter, after performing the pivot, will usually end up facing the back wall or the door of the toilet.

This is clearly the wrong way and should be avoided.

The invention cannot accommodate people like this and they will end up standing there in the wrong pose looking like an idiot.

Those sorts of people should get their act together and learn to do things properly.

The people in large bathrooms or in toilets with irregular wall configurations might still be okay, but the chance of a satisfactory result will probably be reduced. This invention works best, Theo says, in a bog standard toilet.

Once the subject has performed the pivot and is facing a side wall, he or she reaches up and switches on one of the electrical engines. It doesn't matter which one as they are linked. The spooling mechanism of the engine draws toilet paper from the roll and feeds it along a guiding channel framed by a number of wire supports extending up from the floor.

The toilet paper passes from the toilet roll attached to one wall across the floor of the toilet at a height of approximately two feet. This height may be adjusted – Theo thinks of everything. The toilet paper reaches the other wall and is fed through the spooling mechanism to a bin where it may be collected for disposal or reuse.

The subject lifts one leg over the toilet paper which is now moving like a conveyor belt from one wall to the other and lowers himself, or herself, appropriately.

While the hands-free toilet paper dispenser does its vital work the subject may continue doing whatever it is they were doing, or they can simply perch there and marvel at Theo's genius and the wonders of modern technology.

Amazing.

Yep, amazing.

One Saturday morning, after much preliminary tinkering, Theo installed this invention in the upstairs toilet he shares with his sister Filomena. When it was finally operational he called me, Leroy and Toby over and we all gave it a shot.

I have to say that it worked brilliantly for me and Leroy was similarly impressed. Theo pushed it to its limits by having his morning bowl of cereal in there and when he emerged he gave it the big double thumbs up.

Then Toby went in.

I'm not entirely sure what happened in there but when Toby came out he didn't look as enthusiastic as the rest of us. In fact, he looked more than a little worried. Before we could question him, though, Filomena came running up the stairs and told us all to clear off. It was an emergency, she said, and we'd better clear the deck.

Rack off, in other words.

Vamoose.

So we all removed ourselves into Theo's bedroom and Filomena, who can be tremendously scary sometimes, went into the toilet and slammed the door closed.

All of a sudden Toby began to look really worried. He went pale, in fact.

I started to get that awful sinking feeling and opened my mouth to ask Toby what had happened. Before I could speak the sound of Filomena's voice cut me off.

"What the heck?" we heard her say through the door after she had locked it behind her. Then came the horrified scream, followed shortly after by the roar of anger.

"WHAT THE HECK!"

This was followed by lots of coughing and choking noises and then some loud bangs and thumps. It sounded as though Filomena was having a fight in there.

Toby went even paler, if that was possible, and he grunted something we couldn't hear. Then he shouldered us aside and ran out of Theo's bedroom.

We heard his heavy footsteps thumping down the stairs, probably two or three at a time, followed by the slamming of the front door. Then we heard his footsteps receding rapidly into the distance.

All of a sudden things were starting to look very grim.

Theo, Leroy and I stood rooted to the spot, unsure of what to do. The noise in the toilet suddenly ceased and there was silence.

"What do we do?" said Leroy. "Should we run?"

Theo opened his mouth to reply but by then it was too late. The monster had been unleashed.

The next few minutes, I have to confess, are somewhat of a blur for me. One minute the three of us were standing in a state of great confusion and indecision in Theo's bedroom. The next minute Filomena burst out of the toilet screaming and furious. She flew straight into Theo's room and then bodies were being thrown everywhere, furniture and possessions were being smashed up and people were yelling and wailing.

Theo was singled out for special attention and was on the receiving end of a flurry of slaps and punches. Leroy and I were cornered and copped several kicks and a vicious Chinese burn. It was both humiliating and agonising.

Then, as quickly as she had come in, Filomena was gone. As was Theo's latest invention. It had been torn down, ripped to pieces and thrown out of the toilet window.

Silence returned to the Thorne household. We picked ourselves up and gingerly took stock of the damage to Theo's bedroom and our persons.

"We should have followed Toby," moaned Leroy. "As soon as he took off we should have bolted."

"He should have warned us," grumbled Theo, rubbing his head.

"I think he tried to," I replied, inspecting the damage to my forearm caused by Filomena's savage attack. It was a most livid red colour and throbbed painfully.

Among Theo's family and friends, Filomena is notorious for her Chinese burns. They are quick and brutal, and Filomena has never been known to show mercy. These Chinese burns are a strange and terrible phenomenon and I have experienced them on a number of occasions – usually through no fault of my own.

I find it hard to explain, but I hate them and I fear them, but I get a strange thrill of excitement at the same time whenever I receive one.

Theo can't understand this irrationality and dismisses it as some kind of mental aberration or hysteria. When I mentioned it to Toby once, though, he nodded slowly and seemed to understand. Theo's father, who happened to be passing at the time and heard our conversation, gave a loud snort.

"Get used to it, you little dweebs," he said. "Women just love dishing out the pain." Then he started pointing at us and laughing.

Yes, when she was angry or riled up, which was really quite common, Filomena could be very scary indeed. Very, very scary.

Some time later, after we had helped Theo bandage his eye and retrieved the remnants of his invention from the garden, we went looking for Toby.

We managed to find him back at his house hiding in the shed in his back garden. After repeatedly reassuring him that we were not followed we asked him what had happened in the toilet.

"I don't know," he squeaked, as his cheeks started to wobble, "It was all going so well. The paper was going from wall to wall, doing its job, and when I twisted around to get a better look I think I must have bumped one of the engines. I didn't mean to. It was an accident, honest. Then the paper started going backwards, out of the bin and back through the spools and the wire frames towards the toilet roll. I didn't know what to do. I switched it off and came out. I was going to ask Theo how I could fix it all up when his sister came up. She shouldn't have gone into the toilet, I hadn't really finished."

Toby peered out through the shed door nervously.

"You're quite sure that Filomena didn't follow you?" he asked. "She's not around here anywhere? It's just that it might have been a bit messy in there."

Chapter 3

Hidden Sequences

I have just reread the last bunch of pages. As I did it struck me that some of you may have been surprised to learn that Theo was able to spend more than forty dollars on his portable alien detector invention and then just give it away.

Forty dollars!

Now I don't know about you, but I have never, in my whole life, had forty dollars at my disposal to do with completely as I wished. Occasionally I might get forty or fifty dollars on my birthday or as a Christmas present, but my parents always keep a close eye on how that gets spent, and more often than not some of it ends up being deposited in the bank.

Such a waste.

If I was to spend that kind of money on something and then give it away, even temporarily, I would get a sound telling off and probably a whack for good measure.

Theo, however, never seems to be short of resources when it comes to his inventions. It's a different story at school sometimes, when he'll try to scrounge a couple of dollars off one of us in order to buy an ice cream, but he's never been short of funds for equipment or research. Clearly his parents have something to do with that.

Also, I'm pretty certain that the flow of available money stems, in large part, from Theo's groundbreaking work on his exploding mobile phone invention (groundbreaking – that's a good one, ha ha!).

Theo never talks about his access to this supply of money, not even to me, and so far I haven't asked him about it. Apparently, though, he is also forbidden to talk to anybody about his exploding mobile phone invention.

Forbidden!

Expressly forbidden!

This order has come from his mother and also, you may be surprised to hear, from the government.

It's true, I swear it.

Theo has been expressly forbidden, by both his mother and the government, to talk about his exploding mobile phone invention to anybody.

Amazing eh?

But he's told me all about it.

I mean, really. Trying to stop Theo from talking about one of his inventions is like trying to stop an elephant stampede with a picture of a mouse. Impossible. And as nobody has forbidden me to talk about anything to anybody, I might as well tell you.

Theo's exploding mobile phone invention is probably his most successful invention to date, and it came about through his interest in hidden sequences. I expect you're familiar with those. If not, you should be.

Hidden sequences. You know – hidden sequences!

Come on, you must have heard about the *express elevator hidden sequence*. You know the one I mean. It goes something like this:

1. You get into a crowded elevator.

2. You hold down the 'close doors' button.

3. You press the floor you want to go to.

4. The elevator bypasses the floors everyone else has selected.

5. The elevator goes straight to the floor you selected.

6. You laugh and exit the elevator.

7. The other people say, 'Who was that amazing kid?'

Pretty cool, isn't it?

I have to admit, though, that I've never been brave enough to try the *express elevator hidden sequence*.

For a start, there aren't many buildings with elevators in my part of town. And when I do finally get into an elevator I usually forget the sequence or are too slow or someone else presses the buttons or whatever.

One day when I get into an elevator and I'm the only one in there I'll try it. However, I have heard that there are many individuals out there – police officers, firemen, people busting to go to the toilet – who swear by the *express elevator hidden sequence* and use it all the time.

Other well-known hidden sequences include the *hotel safe hidden sequence,* which will open any hotel safe, and the *suitcase combination lock hidden sequence,* which will open any suitcase or briefcase that uses a combination lock. This sequence also works with combination bicycle locks.

Knowledge of this particular hidden sequence has proven very useful to both Theo and me. This is usually when one or both of us are bored with walking or we're tired and we need to borrow a bicycle that someone has inconveniently locked to a pole, fence or bike rack.

Another interesting hidden sequence, but not one that I have ever used, is the *petrol bowser hidden sequence*. This one will fill a car's petrol tank but only clock up a maximum of ten or fifteen dollars on the display.

I think this hidden sequence might be a bit illegal, though, as it was created by workers on the petrol bowser factory floor without the manufacturer's knowledge or approval. It's a handy sequence to know, though, if you have a car and you're fed up with the high price of petrol, or if you'd rather use your petrol money to buy a new skateboard or some chewing gum.

Also handy to know, and employed many times in practice by Theo and the rest of us, is the *vending machine hidden sequence*. What you have to do with this one is enter the hidden sequence into the keypad of any vending machine. Then you enter the code for the desired drink or snack and then – voila – it's yours, free of charge. This hidden sequence, wonderful though it may be, is probably illegal as well. Like most of the good stuff.

I was going to let you know what the *vending machine hidden sequence* is so you could try it out for yourself. But I think that maybe I'd better not. I don't want to get you into trouble. And far more importantly, I don't want to get *me* into trouble. So you are probably better off leaving those vending machines alone. Unless you fancy a spell in jail or whatever it is that they do to juvenile criminals. Make them eat soap or write *I will be a good citizen* ten thousand times or whatever.

Anyway, it was Theo's interest in these hidden sequences, and there are loads and loads more of them, that led to his experiments last year with mobile phones.

Now Theo hates mobile phones. He loves calculators, computers and gaming consoles, but he hates mobile phones. Every kid we know either has one or wants one but Theo really, really hates them.

Mobile phones just steal a kid's freedom, Theo says. Despite what you might think they don't give you any freedom, no way. They take it away. Why would anyone want to be contactable by their parents at any time and in any place? Where's the freedom in that? Theo just couldn't understand it.

Theo's got a point, but my parents won't allow me to have a mobile phone at present so the issue doesn't really concern me too much. I wouldn't mind one, though, if I'm to be absolutely honest. Regardless of what Theo says about them.

Anyway, back to Theo's exploding mobile phone invention. It's another good one.

For some time Theo had toyed with several ideas for automating the destruction of mobile phones. After carefully weighing the pros and cons of each idea he eventually settled on one that he would trial. He decided to plant thin sachets of baking soda and vinegar with a small triggering mechanism under the casing of his sister Filomena's brand new phone. Then he would dial her number and enter the hidden sequence he had devised.

When this happened the vinegar and baking soda would mix together and be agitated and the phone would explode in a mass of foam and slime.

Brilliant, isn't it?

We thought it was a cracking idea.

Theo gathered together the materials and components he needed, and then when Filomena was off playing tennis he managed to get hold of her phone. After making all of the necessary adjustments to the phone he managed to replace it unobserved then settled on a date and time for the trial to occur. As that moment drew near he called me (on the landline, of course) and invited me to his house to observe and record the proceedings.

Filomena had only had the phone for a few days and happened to be showing it off to her friends Emily and Mai at the designated time of eruption. The girls were sitting on the trampoline in the Thorne's back garden discussing its various features. Theo and I were upstairs in his bedroom with his father's mobile phone. We could hear the girls' conversation clearly drifting up through the window.

"Ready to go?" said Theo, with a devilish smile on his face.

I took a quick look out of the window. Filomena and Emily were sitting with their backs against the trampoline's netting and Mai was lying flat on her belly in the middle of the rubber circle.

"You bet," I replied. "Go for it."

Theo sniggered then dialled Filomena's number as we watched them from the window. When her mobile phone rang her father's phone number flashed up on its screen.

"Oh, boring, it's just my stupid dad," we could hear her

say to her friends, and she pressed the button to answer the call.

"Hello? Hello?"

Theo smirked and keyed in his hidden sequence. There was a pause, then another "Hello?" from Filomena, and then a loud shriek as the mobile phone started oozing and bubbling.

Filomena dropped the phone and as it hit the trampoline its casing exploded sending a spray of warm foam over the three girls. They all screamed in horror and leaped off the trampoline, then ran around the back garden in a wild panic clawing at the muck on their skin and clothes.

"It's burning my skin," we heard Mai screech. "It must be acid, it's burning me. It's on my face and hair. It's burning me up."

Then Mai let out a loud, heartrending wail. Things must have taken a turn for the worse. *Oh no . . . oh no, it's on my new shoes too!*

Hearing that, the other girls forgot about their hair and faces and focused on their clothing and accessories.

Filomena's mobile phone was left to die a slow death on the trampoline in a messy puddle of grey and white froth.

"Wow," we could hear Emily say breathlessly after the girls had realized that the foam wasn't acidic, had quietened down and stopped running around.

"That was intense. Like, *so* intense. How did he do that? Your dad must be like, really angry with you or something."

"That wasn't my father," replied Filomena. "That wasn't my father at all. That was my little brat of a brother, and he is going to suffer big time!"

The last part of Filomena's sentence was a high pitched

yell, loaded with venom and directed towards the window we were skulking behind. Theo gulped and shrank away from the window. I decided that it was probably a good time to head home.

So I did.

Although Filomena would probably have disagreed, Theo's exploding mobile phone invention had to be counted as a major success. When Theo's father heard about it he laughed so much that a spray of coffee came out of both his nostrils and covered the passport application he was witnessing for a university colleague. Mr Thorne, who wasn't that keen on mobile phones either, thought that the invention was an absolute ripper.

Theo's mother was impressed as well, but not so much by the fizzing phone trick, which she thought was immature and wasteful. No, she was more interested in the hidden sequence that Theo had used to set off his mobile phone bomb.

Theo's mother was so interested, in fact, that after giving Theo a good telling off for destroying Filomena's phone, Mrs Thorne congratulated him on his enterprise and ingenuity. Then she quizzed him long and hard about his methods.

Theo explained all that he had done and gave his mother a detailed description of how his sequence worked. On the following day his mother took Theo's ideas to the research institute where she worked and talked to some people there about them.

That was when things started to happen.

Unfortunately I wasn't around to witness the following incident – I was at home and it was way past my bedtime –

but Theo filled me in on the details and he swore that every word he spoke was true.

Several nights after Mrs Thorne had taken Theo's ideas to her work four black helicopters appeared to come out of nowhere and landed in the street outside Theo's house.

As I said before, I was in bed at the time and while I heard the helicopters – like just about everyone else in the neighbourhood – I did not see them. Due to the lateness of the hour I don't think that many people did see them, apart from the Thorne family and maybe a few nosy night-owls.

Old Mr Grigoroff, who lived in a small house across the road from Theo, was one person who did, though. Mr Grigoroff had served with valour during the Korean War but was now, according to Mr Thorne, completely off his rocker.

Anyway, upon hearing the helicopters Mr Grigoroff came charging out of his garage in a short orange dressing gown waving a loaded shotgun around his head. He was steamed up big time and ready to rumble.

It seemed that years and years of pent up frustration and resentment at government mismanagement and political correctness had finally taken its toll on old Mr Grigoroff. He was ready to snap and the sight of four sinister helicopters landing on the street in front of his house and scaring his two Burmese cats was enough to send him right over the edge.

Taking aim at one of the helicopters, Grigoroff pulled the trigger of his shotgun and blew apart his letterbox. Cursing ferociously, he planted his feet solidly on his tidy front lawn, took careful aim and let them have the other barrel. His shot was better this time.

Much better.

It flew straight and true towards the cockpit of the nearest helicopter. The pilot's mouth was seen to open with a contorted but silent: *"Noooooo!"*

Fortunately for the pilot, Mr Grigoroff's van was positioned directly between the shotgun's muzzle and the helicopter's cockpit. Its passenger door took the full force of the blast and the wing mirror vanished in a shower of sparks.

Grigoroff was incensed. *"Sabotage!"* he screamed, his face purple and bulging, *"Government sabotage!!"*

Mr Grigoroff was now temporarily out of ammunition and while he fumbled in his pockets for more shells two men leaped from the second helicopter and subdued him. Having contemplated then dismissed the idea of shooting him where he stood (the paperwork in such cases was horrendous), the first man sprang to Mr Grigoroff's side and flicked his glasses off his nose, rendering him sightless. Then he grabbed his left wrist and twisted it gently up behind his back.

The other man grabbed the shotgun and in the blink of an eye completely dismantled the weapon, dropping its 26 components onto Mr Grigoroff's immaculate front lawn. Then he finished the elderly combatant off with a quick tap of his foot to the back of Mr Grigoroff's knees.

Defeated and disillusioned, but by no means dishonoured, Mr Grigoroff slipped to the ground and pretended to fall asleep.

Theo filled me in on that particular incident and all of the other details later. He had seen it all from one of the upstairs front windows.

After taking care of Mr Grigoroff, who apparently was known to them, a group of heavily armed and muscular men in dark uniforms had entered Theo's house. After several minutes they gently escorted Mrs Thorne outside and into one of the helicopters. Then they all took off and flew away, leaving the neighbourhood peaceful once more, but wondering what the heck had just happened.

After a day and two nights Mrs Thorne returned home, exhausted but unharmed. Although she was forbidden to say anything to anyone about where she had been and what had happened she could not keep the smile off her face.

Not long after that Filomena's ruined mobile phone was replaced and Theo's mother was promoted at work. What passed for normality returned to the Thorne household. Then a few days later Theo had more funds at his disposal for his inventions and Mrs Thorne had a new convertible Maserati in the garage to go with the Porsche she used for work.

Although Mrs Thorne had been sworn to secrecy by the men in the black helicopters she couldn't help but tell Theo some of what had resulted from his ideas. She didn't bother telling Filomena or her husband. Filomena simply wasn't that interested. Theo's father, who had been engrossed in an episode of Star Trek when the helicopters had landed (during a furious Klingon attack), hadn't even realised that his wife was missing. So Theo's mother only told Theo, and Theo told me. So here's the story.

Mrs Thorne's engineering expertise lies in the related fields of wireless technology and telecommunications, and apparently things can move very quickly in those industries. Particularly when lots of money is at stake or when men in black helicopters get involved.

Theo explained to me that there are about thirty companies around the world that manufacture mobile phones, and that the top five of those companies make around two-thirds of the total number of phones sold.

Which is a lot of mobile phones.

Especially when you consider that close to six billion of the things have been sold in the past twenty years.

Boring, I hear you say, this is getting very boring.

Don't worry, I hear you. I thought the same as well. But it does get less boring, so please be patient.

I'm sure you know that the big problem in the world today, apart from reality television, the destruction of the environment and all of the economic woes, is terrorism. Individuals or groups of people intent on leaving a trail of death and destruction across the globe. You know that and I know that. We all know that. But then Theo told me something that I didn't know.

Apparently, governments that are taking action against terrorism realised a long time ago that while it can be very difficult to track individuals, tracking manufactured items such as cars, refrigerators and mobile phones is much, much easier.

It seems that a huge industry has sprung up around the planting of tiny electronic tags in everything that is built and sold. Those tags can emit radio signals that may be picked up by a reader device, recorded and stored. This technology, known as radio-frequency identification (RFID for short), is not really all that new but its use has exploded in recent years and its reach is now being felt in many areas.

For example, you could buy a pair of jeans with one of

the RFID tags sewn into a seam and every time you walked past a reader device the identification number of the tag in your jeans would be recorded and stored in a computer database somewhere. And once it's there that information can be kept forever.

As time progresses these tag readers are being installed in more and more places – shops, cafes, airports, libraries . . . everywhere. They can record what you are wearing and what you are carrying. A tag could be in your shirt, your shoes, your hat or even your underpants, and because they're so small you don't even know it's there.

A tag could be in the book you're carrying or in the packet of mints you have in your pocket. Everything can get read and all of it can be recorded. This information can then be linked to where you bought the product from, where you go, who you are, what you do, and where you live.

Pretty scary, don't you think?

Theo said that this is the way the world is going, and this is the way that terrorists are increasingly being tracked down. Governments no longer try to follow a particular individual. It's too difficult, too expensive and too time-consuming. It's too old-fashioned and it's far too dangerous as well.

Government agents, like most people, get a kick out of fiddling about with the latest technology. It's really all they want to do. They don't want to be out in the cold hiding behind bushes or shadowing violent thugs. They don't want to be stabbed, tortured or put in situations where they might wet their pants or poo their undies in terror. No, they'd rather be sitting in a nice tidy office having a coffee and maybe a biscuit while looking at a computer screen. Doing their stupid social networking, ideally. But if not social networking or playing computer games then doing a bit of work that involves mucking about in some way with technology.

So instead of looking for or following the man, like they used to do in the old days, they concentrate on the technology. They follow the watch on their quarry's wrist, the phone in his pocket, or the spectacles on his head.

The research institute Theo's mother works for happens to do a lot of work in this area. The RFID boffins she spoke to could see straight away that Theo's *mobile phone hidden sequence* was rich with possibility. Which is why they moved so quickly and decisively. They wanted to lock down Theo's ideas before anyone else could get wind of them.

You see, governments have been able to listen in on and record phone conversations for years. They could do that quickly and easily, and are doing it all of the time.

If you have ever been on the phone to someone and heard some strange clicking noises in the earpiece then chances are your conversation was being monitored. This sort of thing was common.

Then when the new RFID technology came along the governments were increasingly able to follow an individual handset as it travelled around the world. So not only listen in to conversations, but track movements as well.

Mobile phone companies have always been able to pinpoint the location of a particular phone, but only when it was turned on. RFID technology allowed a mobile phone to be tracked even when it was off, even if its battery had been removed.

Theo's work took all of this up a notch or two. All that governments now had to do was team up with the mobile phone manufacturers to build a very small and stable explosive device into every mobile phone produced.

Once these had spread throughout the world, whenever a tracked handset and monitored phone conversation indicated that the mobile phone's owner was a terrorist, their number could be dialed. Then Theo's hidden sequence could be keyed in and – boom – another terrorist gets his head blown clean off. Or *her* head.

The scheme was simple but it was thought that it would be very effective. The scheme was so simple, in fact, that the entire process could be automated so that no human intervention was required. Nobody would have to listen to the phone conversations or track the mobile phones. The computers could do it all. The computers could track the phones, listen in, determine that the speaker was probably a terrorist, dial the number and then key in the hidden sequence.

Boom!

Nobody would have to do anything. Once it was all set up, nobody would need to do a single thing.

That's the great thing about an automated system. Once it was switched on, the government agents could remain in their little offices and carry on with their solitaire card game or their stupid social networking. Nobody would be in any danger or inconvenienced. Furthermore, if nobody has to do anything then nobody would have to feel guilty about what was happening out there in the real world.

Theo's mobile phone idea had been brilliant and Theo and his family had been well rewarded. Now, the secret government boffins were going to take Theo's brilliant idea and make it beautiful.

After a while, the terrorists would be living in fear. Mobile phone bombs would be going off every five or ten minutes all over the place and the world would be a far safer place in which to live.

Beautiful.

Chapter 4

The Fabulous Fruit Flinger

All that talk about automated mobile phone bombs has reminded me of another of Theo's interests – automation – and another of his inventions, the automated fruit flinger. This is even more interesting than all of that stuff in the last chapter about RFID, terrorism and exploding mobile phones.

You may recall that at the start of this book I made mention of a certain unpleasant individual by the name of Wayne Galbraith. Yes, you remember him. He is the big orangutan who is in my class at school.

Now, clearly Wayne Galbraith has some kind of gripe against me, which was why he called me a weirdo after school that day. But I'm not the only one who has been on the receiving end of one of Wayne Galbraith's jibes. Theo is often being called something unpleasant or offensive by Wayne or one of his cronies. Usually it happens after Theo has deployed one of his inventions against them but that is beside the point.

Leroy and Toby have also been subjected to name-calling. As have most of the rest of our class now that I think about it.

Wayne Galbraith is quite a nasty fellow. Well, we think he is, anyway. When he is not throwing rocks or playing football with his group of idiotic rock-throwing, football-playing friends he likes to wrestle around on the ground, flick elastic bands or spitballs and make up nicknames for people. Those nicknames tend to be stupid and lack imagination, but all of his friends giggle and snigger when he comes up with one.

For example, earlier on this year he came up with the nickname 'Bullet-headed Specco Boy' for Theo, on account of his glasses and the unusually elongated shape of his head. I thought that was far too much of a mouthful to be an effective nickname and so did Theo.

Wayne and his silly chums all giggled away like mad, though, and our teacher, Mr Cranston, thought that it was hilarious. He laughed and laughed when he heard it, clutching his sides and gasping: "O that is wicked . . . that is so wrong . . . ho ho ho," and it was a good few minutes before our lesson on fair play and sensitivity in the playground resumed.

Wayne Galbraith also came up with 'Mini-moy', for Leroy, due to his shorter than average height, and 'Moby' for Toby, on account of his weight, which inclines towards the heavy.

The first is an extremely lame nickname, I'm sure you'll agree. The one for Toby, however, has a small degree of cleverness about it, although I hate to admit it. It is a bit obvious, I suppose, comparing Toby – who is a little on the heavy side – to the famous fictional whale, but on the whole it isn't too bad an effort for someone like Wayne Galbraith.

For some reason Galbraith hasn't yet come up with a nickname for me, and for a good while it appeared that he was ignoring me altogether. That all changed, of course, with the 'weirdo' incident. But that wasn't a nickname; that was more of a direct insult. So I expect that I have made it to his nickname list and no doubt he'll get to me sooner or later.

While Galbraith and his friends can be very annoying with their nicknames and name-calling, up until recently there hadn't been anything too much nastier than that. Sometimes we'd push and shove them and they'd push and shove us back, or vice versa. And to be fair, Galbraith and his friends even have stupid nicknames for each other, which are very frequently in use.

I'm not sure that I've heard a nickname for Galbraith but Paul Viner is known as 'Whiner', and the football-mad Terry Staton – Galbraith's best friend – is just called 'Stinks'. I'm not sure why. Given that some of Galbraith's own friends are lumbered with nicknames like that I suppose we should be thankful with the relatively mild ones he's given to Theo, Leroy and Toby.

Nicknames aside, however, Wayne Galbraith is slowly becoming more of a pest. A while ago he had Toby around the neck at school and they were rolling all over the floor – banging into chair legs, knocking over waste paper bins and colliding with other people sitting on the mat.

I think that Toby might have kicked things off by sticking a pencil into Galbraith's back or something but

Galbraith went overboard with his reaction. Anyway, Toby ended up being really unhappy with the situation but he managed to hold back the tears and keep his pride intact.

"We were only playing," said Galbraith when Miss Nguyen pulled him off. "He wanted me to get him into a paralyzing headlock and show him the neck-busting shoulder slam."

"No I didn't," wheezed Toby. "I've never even heard of it."

"Well, neither have I," countered Galbraith somewhat illogically. Obviously his brain had been affected when his head hit the chair leg for the fourth time.

Miss Nguyen was a compact and pretty teacher who always wore fashionable spectacles and elegant, dark clothing. Softly spoken and gentle, she was one of our favourites, but even so she wasn't going to put up with nonsense like wrestling during religious instruction. Even if it was only play-wrestling.

"Sit down over there, Toby," said Miss Nguyen. "And you sit down over there, Wayne. Such silly behaviour. There'll be no more fighting or wrestling during class, if you don't mind. Please save your paralyzing headlocks and neck-busting shoulder slams for recess or lunch."

With this Miss Nguyen frowned for a moment, obviously thinking back on the aptness of her remark.

"Actually, we'll have no paralyzing headlocks or neck-busting shoulder slams at school at all, if you don't mind," she continued. "Wait until you're off the premises."

Toby was quite upset by this incident and he complained about it on and off for the rest of the day. He also brought it up again after school. We were all sitting on Leroy's front veranda at the time. All of our houses are no more than a ten minute walk away from each other, but Leroy's was kind of in the middle and the quickest for all of us to get to. We often met there after school. He had a couple of really comfortable big couches on the veranda and a seemingly endless supply of soft drink. He also had a huge backyard where he did his star-gazing and sky-watching, and where he practiced his archery, kung fu and knife-throwing. So we all thought that it was a pretty cool place to hang out.

It was Friday afternoon and we were all relaxing and drinking lemonade when Toby said we needed to do something about Wayne Galbraith. Toby had been trying to hypnotize Leroy, and all of a sudden he slammed his hand down on the wooden arm of the couch, making us all jump.

"I can't concentrate. I need a clear head to do this properly."

"What's the problem?" asked Leroy.

"It's that Galbraith kid. He's becoming a real pain. He thinks he's tough and I really hate him. My neck is still sore from that stupid paralyzing headlock."

"Yes," said Leroy, blinking furiously. "We should get him back for that."

"Yeah, we should get him back," agreed Toby. "We should bust his neck and see how he likes it. Hey, why don't you do some of your karate on him?"

Toby was always trying to get Leroy to use his martial arts on someone.

"You know I can't do that," replied Leroy. "It's not allowed. It's too dangerous. And it's kung fu, not karate."

"Well, just do a bit on him. It doesn't have to be the full-blown kung fu. I dunno, just do a bit of kung on him. Not too much, just enough to bust his neck and give him a bit of agony."

"I can't, Toby," said Leroy. "I'd love to, but it's not for use on kids at school. Mr Cranston would flip out if I did some kung fu on Galbraith and he fell down dead. I'd get a black mark for sure and maybe even suspended or something."

"Well, why do you bother doing it then if you can't use it? What a stupid waste of time."

Leroy put his can of lemonade on the table and slumped back on the couch, staring at the veranda ceiling. "One day I'll need to use it," he said. "I can feel it. I don't know when and I don't know why, but when it happens I'll be ready."

"Is it for the aliens?" asked Theo.

"Maybe it is. Maybe it isn't. I don't know." Leroy closed his eyes and yawned.

At that point Leroy's father poked his head out of the front door. He was small and wiry, like Leroy, and he had a thin blond moustache which extended down the sides of his mouth to the edge of his jaw. He was wearing a dirty white singlet and I could see the tattoo he had on his left shoulder. It was a dragon or an eagle or something.

"Leroy, it's time for dinner. Say goodbye to your chums and come inside." His head disappeared back indoors. Leroy sighed and did a loud burp.

To be honest, I'm not really that keen on Leroy's father. I quite like his mother, though, who is a very quiet and gentle lady. Her husband, however, always makes me feel a little uneasy. Whenever I saw him he seemed tired or angry, and he seemed to share Leroy's strange obsession with outer space. He was often muttering things about aliens and using phrases like "taking over the place" and "get rid of them all."

I could see where Leroy's interest in extra-terrestrials came from, but that didn't make it any easier to be around his father. Now and then I caught him looking at us kind of funny, and when we were at their house I sometimes got the feeling that he'd rather we weren't there sitting on his couch or playing in his back garden.

Leroy stood up and stretched. He picked up his empty lemonade can and tossed it into the bin they kept next to the couch.

"Well, I'd better go in, I suppose. Potato and meatballs tonight. Yum. I'll see you later."

The rest of us stood up to go. Leroy opened the door to go inside and Toby, Theo and I started walking down the steps. At the bottom Theo paused. "Hey Leroy," he said. "It's Saturday tomorrow. Come over to my place. You guys too. I may have something we can use on Galbraith."

"Okay," said Leroy. "I've got fencing for an hour at nine, but I'll see you all after that."

"Okay."

The next morning we met up at Theo's house and he took us into the garage. His parents had a triple garage with an alcove attached to the back of it. A large part of the back wall was made of big glass bricks, so during the day the garage was always warm and well lit. Mrs Thorne's Maserati and Porsche occupied two of the car bays, along with her kayak and paddles which were suspended on hooks from the ceiling. Mr Thorne's prized electric bicycle occupied the third bay, accompanied by Theo and Filomena's regular bicycles.

Theo's mother used to have a bicycle – a limited edition BMW mountain bike – but one day she read in a magazine that cycling made women's bottoms bigger. This freaked her out so she gave her bike to her younger and slimmer sister as a graduation present.

Mr Thorne, Theo and Filomena ridiculed Mrs Thorne for this, claiming it was totally unproven and that as an engineer and a scientist she should know better. Academic studies were then located and examined, and research findings scrutinized, until Mrs Thorne was forced to concede that not only was the original assertion unproven, it was probably incorrect. Despite this capitulation, however, a tiny sliver of doubt remained in her mind and while that doubt persisted she could no longer run the risk of climbing upon a bicycle.

The alcove at the back of the garage was Theo's domain. It was where he did his 'dirty' work, as opposed to the 'clean' stuff he did in his bedroom. Theo's parents were quite particular about order and cleanliness, especially when it came to the interior of their house. As such they were adamant that nothing dirty should be going on in Theo's bedroom. So he used the alcove in the garage quite a lot when he was working on his inventions, especially when he was using chemicals, preparing explosions or smashing things up.

After spending some time lounging about in the open-topped Maserati and admiring the Porsche, which we did each time we visited the garage, and then pouring scorn on the electric bicycle, which we always did as well, we moved our attention to the alcove. There, on the long wooden bench, stood one of Theo's more recent inventions.

It was very small and made of wood and metal. In some ways it resembled a miniature medieval engine-of-war. You know, one of those catapults they used in the olden days to fling huge boulders or dead cows over castle walls. Theo's invention, however, was much smaller and could easily sit in the palm of your hand. Leroy leaned right over it until his nose almost knocked it over.

"Great," he muttered. "I've been wanting to see one of these for years. What is it?"

"This, my friends, is my latest invention. It is called the fabulous fruit flinger." Theo gave a little bow and then picked it up.

"Wonderful," said Leroy. "So it flings fruit. I don't see anything too fabulous about that. I can fling fruit myself. Why would I need a machine? And it's such a little machine. That's not going to be able to fling much fruit."

This was true. The fruit-holding part of the fabulous fruit flinger was rather small. It was a little cup, and probably about half the size of my thumbnail. And that's the nail on my left thumb too, which is a bit smaller than the one on my right.

Theo was not perturbed by Leroy's questions.

"With this invention," said Theo, "it's not what it does that's important, it's how it does it. Let me demonstrate."

I knew this was coming. There's nothing Theo loves more than showing people how smart he is or demonstrating his inventions.

Theo had come prepared. He pulled a couple of old tomatoes out of a bag on the bench and waved the smaller one up in the air.

"Observe. Here we have a standard, if slightly scungy,

tomato. First we set the fabulous fruit flinger's firing mechanism, like so. Then we carefully gouge a piece of pulp out of this tomato and load it into the fabulous fruit flinger's fruit-holding cup, like so. There . . . done. The fabulous fruit flinger's firing mechanism has a delayed action, so now we wait."

Theo placed the fabulous fruit flinger on the bench and took a pace back. We all stood there and watched it. The fabulous fruit flinger seemed to be vibrating ever so slightly.

"What you're seeing now is its latent energy starting to transform," said Theo, who was beginning to get excited. "This baby is about to go kinetic and blow."

To my eyes the fruit-holding cup, if it blew the way it looked as though it would, was pointed in our direction.

"Hey Theo," I said. "Is that thing aimed at us?"

Theo chuckled. "It is, but don't be alarmed. Don't be a pansy. No need to wet your pants. We're quite safe here."

We all stood our ground, holding our breath, while the intensity of the fabulous fruit flinger's vibrations increased visibly. Then all of a sudden the thing went off with a loud snap. One minute we could see the clump of tomato sitting on the little cup, then in the next instant the contraption jumped, the cup was on the opposite side of the flinger and the tomato was gone.

"What happened?" asked Toby, who had blinked at just the wrong moment.

"Success!" shouted Theo.

"But what happened?" repeated Toby, oblivious to the splodge of tomato splattered on the front of his white skivvy. "Where'd it go?"

"It's there, Toby," said Leroy, pointing at his belly.

"What?"

"There, you bozo."

"Blimey," said Toby. "I think I must have blinked when it went off. I didn't see it. I didn't even feel it."

Leroy started laughing. "I didn't see it either and I had my eyes wide open. That thing is deadly. It went like a bullet!"

Theo smiled and moved back to the bench. "That's only the half of it. Flinging a chunk of fruit is easy. Any moron could do that. Now I will demonstrate the clever bit. Toby, go and stand over there."

"What, here?"

"Yes."

Toby went as directed and stood near the front of the garage, on the other side of the three bicycles. Theo picked up the other tomato, the larger one, and cut a hole in the top. He scooped out some of its messy contents then set the fabulous fruit flinger's firing mechanism. Then he pushed the machine into the tomato and covered it, cup as well, with pulp. The fabulous fruit flinger could no longer be seen.

"Ready?" shouted Theo.

Toby put his hands up. "Wait! Why am I here, Theo? Why I am here?"

"Too late," yelled Theo, and drew back his arm.

"Stop!" screamed Toby, but Theo wasn't listening. A split-second later the tomato was airborne and tracing an arc through the air in Toby's direction.

"Stop!" screamed Toby again, but at the tomato this time.

The tomato wasn't listening, either. It continued on its

path towards him, and Toby watched it with wide eyes and a stricken look on his face. He wanted to run, or leap to one side, but all of a sudden he was unable to move. His body had frozen and his feet felt like heavy concrete blocks sunk into holes in the ground and covered with tiny pebbles. It was as though the flying tomato had hypnotized him, like a deadly snake about to strike.

All hope lost, Toby opened his mouth to scream again but then, to his huge relief, the tomato rapidly lost height and fell with a soft plop onto the ground a few feet in front of him.

"You missed," said Toby, triumphantly.

"Don't move," shouted Theo.

"Why not?" asked Toby, but he remained where he was. By now he was crouching slightly, with his arms held away from his torso. He was sweating and his body was rigid. He looked as though he had just been told he was standing on an anti-tank mine.

A second ticked by. Perspiration beaded Toby's brow. I saw a drop of sweat emerge from his shorts and trickle down the inside of his left leg into the top of his sock. At least I hoped it was sweat. Once again we waited, our eyes locked onto the tomato, all of us holding our breath and trying our hardest not to blink.

The snap, when it came, was more muffled than before but the end result was far more spectacular. The tomato gave a jump and we could see the small ball of pulp go streaking towards Toby. It hit him on the side of his chin and left an ugly red smear on his face. Toby had seen it coming and flinched backwards. The heel of one shoe caught the toe of the other and he lost his balance, toppling over. With his arms windmilling theatrically he crashed into the garage door with a terrific clatter then slumped to the concrete floor and lay still.

"He's dead!" yelled Leroy. "Cripes, Theo, you've killed Toby! You've bumped him off. His mum's going to go absolutely mental."

"Rubbish," said Theo. "He's not dead."

Theo walked over to where Toby lay on the garage floor. Toby remained motionless. A tiny stream of tomato trickled slowly from his mouth.

"Toby," said Theo. "Toby, are you okay?" He leaned over and touched Toby on the shoulder. There was no response.

"Oh no," said Theo, his voice cracking and then rising in intensity. "Oh no. Oh no, no, noooo . . . I think that he may actually be . . . I think that he *is* . . . oh, no he isn't, he's okay."

Toby moaned and sat up. He touched his face lightly then looked down at the tomato dripping from his chin onto his chest. "Looks like you got me good, Theo."

"Looks like it," replied Theo. "Sorry about the skivvy."

"That's okay. I'll say it was your mum's fault."

"Thanks."

"No problem."

While Toby was getting to his feet and tenderly dusting himself down Leroy picked the mutilated tomato up and pulled out the fabulous fruit flinger.

"Theo, how do you aim this thing when it's inside the fruit?"

"Eh?"

"How did you make it hit Toby?"

"How do you aim it?"

"Yes."

"Well, the base of the flinger is weighted, of course, so it's self-righting. All you need to do is pack the flinger straight into the fruit. Then when you throw it you have to make sure that it doesn't deviate from that line. It takes a bit of practice, but when you know what you're doing you can get a straight shot nine times out of ten."

"Oh."

"What do you think? Pretty nifty, eh? Chuck a rotten tomato at someone, he thinks you've missed and has a good laugh, and then splat! Right in the face, if you're lucky."

"I like it," said Leroy. "I like it a lot. It's flipping fantastic. Hey, shall we use it on Galbraith? Can we use it on Galbraith, Theo? What do you think, Toby?"

"It's brilliant," said Toby, wiping the last of the tomato from his chin. "This is perfect. It's just what we need."

"I thought you'd approve," said Theo.

Toby gave a slow, wicked smile. He nodded slowly a couple of times and rubbed his hands together in glee.

"This is unreal. It's amazing. Thank you, Theo."

"You're welcome, Toby."

Chapter 5

The Magician

Toby's mood improved enormously after Theo's fabulous fruit flinger demonstration. The thought of Wayne Galbraith copping it squarely in the face from Theo's invention lifted his spirits considerably. As we made our way back to his house Toby kept clutching his sides and giggling to himself.

We had parted company with Theo and Leroy after a few more experimental shots with the fabulous fruit flinger. Theo had some kind of an extended family lunch in the city that he was expected to attend and Leroy was hoping that his father might take him bowling or to the rifle range. So Toby and I said goodbye to them and started walking home. Toby lived nine doors away from me so we often saw each other. He was probably my second best friend after Theo, although we didn't hit it off too well when we first met.

Not long after I had become friends with Theo the Thorne family went overseas for a fortnight and I was left alone at school once again. Mrs Thorne needed to present one of her research papers at some big telecommunications conference in Washington, which just happened to coincide with the US national wrestling championships, and although it was during school term time she thought it was a great opportunity to take Theo and Filomena to see the Smithsonian Institution. So off they flew to Washington.

With Theo away I had no one to sit with during recess and lunch. So for a few days I gulped my food down quickly and then went and sat in the library.

One day, however, the teachers were holding some kind of a meeting in there and all of the kids in the library were rounded up and thrown out. There were about eight or nine of us poor souls, covering a range of school years. We spilled out into the playground, sniffling and blinking in the bright light like slaves of old Rome thrust unwillingly onto the freshly raked sands of the amphitheatre. None of us knew where to go or what to do.

I wandered aimlessly around the playground for a while, trying to dodge the balls and the packs of young kids charging about. Then I spied Toby sitting by himself, staring intently at a fork lying on the bench before him. I knew who Toby was because he was in my class, but I had never spoken to him. I walked over to him and sat down on the other side of the bench.

Toby is quite a solid fellow. I have told you already that Wayne Galbraith had nicknamed him 'Moby' but some of the other kids in our class occasionally called him 'Tubs' or 'Fatso.' Apart from being nasty and unimaginative this was also a bit undeserved. Toby wasn't really fat; he just had quite a bulky frame topped by a large head and a round face. His head and face were made more prominent by his hair, which was fair and cut very, very short. Okay, he may have been a little heavier than he should have been but I didn't consider him fat. Ample is probably a better description, although I'm sure he would have preferred the term muscular.

Toby just sat there and stared at his fork. He was ignoring me. He knew I was there but he was deliberately ignoring me. I watched him for a little while and then I could stay silent no longer.

"What's the matter?" I asked. "Did your mum forget to pack your lunch or something?"

There was no response. Toby kept staring at the fork. He was completely immobile. In fact, he was more than completely immobile, he was rigid. It was as though his body was being subjected from all sides to some incredible, invisible pressure. I could see a trickle of sweat rolling down from the hair at his temple. All of this surprised me as it was a cool day and he wasn't doing anything apart from sitting on a bench looking at a fork.

"Are you all right?" I asked again. If I was a veterinarian or had some kind of medical training I might have suspected he was having a stroke or a heart attack or something. I don't know anything about biology or medicine though. So I just sat there and started to suspect that the problem might just be that he was an idiot.

I was about to open my mouth again to ask him if this was so when he beat me to it by opening his.

"Go away," he murmured quietly through a slit in the corner of his mouth. "I'm busy."

I wasn't having that.

"What do you mean, you're busy? You're just sitting here. How can you be busy? What are you doing, being busy looking at a fork? Being busy sweating?"

"Go away," he said again through clenched teeth.

I had only just sat down and I wasn't going anywhere. I could sit there if I wanted to. He didn't own the bench. Besides, I was curious about his behaviour.

"Look, I'm just trying to be friendly," I said. I was mystified by his attitude. "I saw you here by yourself and I thought that I'd sit down as well."

"Go away," he said once more. The strain on his face was apparent and it looked to be taking its toll. "At the moment I don't want anyone being friendly. I don't want any friends."

"Well, that's great because neither do I, really. But I just want to sit here. Where's the harm in that?"

Silence fell across the pair of us. The rest of the school playground was a sea of movement. There were kids everywhere. Talking, laughing, shouting, throwing balls and throwing food. Some were walking, some were running and some were falling flat on their faces. Well, one girl was falling flat on her face.

Across the quadrangle, someone had thoughtlessly left their bag lying in the middle of the corridor. The girl had come belting around the corner at a tremendous pace and tripped over it. I could see her tumble end over end, her legs cutting through the air like a gymnast doing a high-speed cartwheel. The exhibition ended with the girl lying in a crumpled heap against the water fountain. One of her shoes had been flung off by the force of the impact and lay atop a row of lockers.

Mr Cranston, who was on playground duty, happened to be walking in that direction and saw it all. He let out a giant guffaw and started slapping his thigh. When the girl started to wail I turned my attention back to Toby.

There was no further movement from him. Even his trickle of sweat had stopped, just on the end of his chin. I watched it, fascinated, but it refused to drop. The playground continued to heave around us, but our bench was an island of immobility, a frozen wasteland, a place where all time and activity seemed to stand still. The spell was broken by a low moan from Toby, followed by a sharp crack like thunder from the seat of his pants.

"What the heck was that?" I exclaimed, as Toby emerged from his trance and slumped backwards, nearly falling off the bench in the process.

"Close, so close," moaned Toby. "It was so close. It almost moved, I could almost feel it move."

By this time I was starting to get a bit concerned. Was he always like this? Maybe coming and sitting down here hadn't been such a good idea after all.

"Toby," I suggested gently, "if you're feeling things move then perhaps you should be heading to the toilet."

Toby looked at me then, and it was probably the first time he had ever done so. It was a look heavy with reproach and disgust.

"The fork, you pinhead. I nearly made the fork move."

Yes, another example of name-calling. What is it with this place?

"I do have a name, you know. You really shouldn't be going around calling people pinheads. Especially when someone is trying to be friendly to you and especially when that someone is me. It isn't nice, you know."

"I already told you, I don't want people being friendly towards me. Are you thick? I told you I don't want another friend. I don't want any more friends. I don't want you for a friend."

"Well I don't want you for a friend, either."

"Good."

"Fine. Let's just sit here not being friends."

"Fine."

"Let's sit here being enemies."

"Fine."

I was finding this Toby guy really annoying and I was starting to think that maybe he felt the same way about me. So we just sat there and looked at each other. The fork lay between us, motionless. Toby started sweating again, and every now and then I saw him take a sneaky glance down at the table. I think that while he was sitting here pretending to do nothing he was really trying to move the fork again, on the sly.

This Toby was a sneaky devil.

After a while the siren rang and we got up and made our way back to class. We walked together but no more words were said.

When school was over for the day I grabbed my bag and followed Toby through the gate. I knew he lived near me – I had seen him mucking around in his front garden a few times and once when it was raining I saw him run out to the letter box in his underpants to retrieve the mail. I think that because it was raining he thought that nobody would be around to see him. But I was standing under the bus shelter just up the road, waiting for a break in the clouds, and just at that moment a people-mover carrying about six kids from school drove by as well. So we all had a good laugh at him then and for several days afterwards at school.

Outside the school gate I caught up with Toby and slowly we walked back to our street together. I asked him again what he had been doing with the fork but politely avoided any mention of the thunderclap I had heard coming from his backside.

Although he still claimed that he didn't want me to be his friend, and I told him that I'd rather be dead than be any friend of his, he started to talk a little, and by the end of the walk I knew a bit more about him and he knew a bit more about me.

At lunchtime, Toby had been trying to make the fork move using nothing but his will and the power of his mind. This was a particular ambition of his and he practiced it every day. He was convinced that one day he would be able to move objects by mind power alone. Toby told me that his father had been an accomplished magician and that certain inexplicable powers had long been known to run down that side of his family.

Toby had always wanted to be a magician, like his father, and one day he told his father that he would also like to be able to move things with his mind. On hearing that, Toby's father grabbed his son by his shoulders and encouraged him to recognise and articulate his dream, and then to chase after it.

"You go for it, my boy," Toby's father had boomed. He had a lovely deep voice, apparently.

"Too many people sit on their rumps doing nothing. They're too afraid to take a chance and they waste their lives. You chase that dream down and make it real. You can do it, I know you can. If you want it bad enough, you can do it."

Toby's father had been waving his arms expansively as he spoke and beer from the bottle in his hand had flown through the air and spattered onto the floor and wall. Some of it went on Toby as well.

"I chased my dreams," Toby's father went on, with even greater fervour. He was on his feet by then and his arms were flailing about wildly. Beer was going everywhere. "For years I chased my dreams. How I strived and strived. And look at the magic I've made! Look at the magic I've made!"

Obviously all his efforts and recollections had exhausted him, for at that point he collapsed back into his armchair and took a long swig of what remained in his bottle. Then he closed his eyes and rubbed his hand across his face.

As well as being a magician, Toby's father was, by all accounts, an excitable and emotional man, and on that occasion his emotions seemed to get the better of him.

Since then Toby had been focusing his mind and attempting the movement of objects using nothing but the force of his willpower and the energy of his brain. Three years he had been at it, practicing every day for fifteen or twenty minutes at a time.

On one day, after some intense and exhausting practice, his level of enthusiasm shot through the roof. He had been working hard on a piece of paper, trying to get some movement across the flat surface of the kitchen table. All of a sudden the paper moved.

Toby leaped to his feet and nearly wet his pants with excitement. After running around the room yelling he calmed himself and sat down to try it once more. He took a deep breath to help refocus his mind, and as he exhaled the paper moved again. The edge closest to Toby lifted slightly and the paper slid smoothly across the polished table. Another breath, another movement.

Oh.

Toby was disappointed, but not disheartened. He knew he had to keep trying, and resolved to try harder and harder until he had achieved his goal.

In addition to this mind power, or telekinesis, as it's more properly known, Toby also practiced magic and hypnosis. These were the other powers that Toby really wanted to master. After all, his father had been a magician, so why not him?

One of Toby's earliest memories was of his father showing him a magic trick using two coins and a ribbon, and since that day Toby was hooked. As soon as his father returned home from his day job in the foundry Toby would ask him to do some magic and his father often obliged. One day the coin trick, the next day a card trick – it didn't matter how many times Toby saw them. He never grew tired of his father's showmanship, his sleight of hand, and magic.

Magic.

Amused by his young son's interest and eagerness, Toby's father took a book out of the local library and grew more and more ambitious. He started cutting things in half and making them whole. He transported bottle tops from beneath one upturned cup to another. He pulled sweets from behind Toby's ear and a big bunch of flowers from a hat or a lunchbox.

This was a wonderful period in Toby's life. It was exciting and endlessly entertaining. The kitchen table was his father's preferred location for these magical activities but if Toby's mother had been yelling too much they would go and sit under the tree in the back garden. There Toby's father would make blades of grass appear mysteriously between his fingers and guide nails through solid chunks of wood. His father's favourite magic trick, though, was making things disappear and then reappear. Coins, watches, pebbles, salt and pepper shakers – Toby's father made them all disappear. Then they would reappear in the strangest and most unexpected places.

Toby was enthralled by his father's skills. He loved the words he used to build the tension, the elegant way that he moved his hands, and his ability to perform the impossible right in front of him. Toby's days were filled with magic. It was wonderful.

Of course, wonderful doesn't last forever. I expect you know that. You've been around long enough to know how the world tends to work. I also expect you know what's coming next.

Correct.

One day, just over a year ago and without any warning, Toby's father – the magician – made himself disappear. He didn't do it in front of Toby, who was at school at the time, nor in front of Toby's mother, who was at work. He did it when he was by himself, when there was no one else around to see him and no one else around to stop him.

Toby's father had dropped him off at school that morning and instead of immediately driving away as he normally did he watched his son walk all of the way from the car to the door of his classroom. Toby was unaware that his father had lingered but after leaving his bag outside on the rack he turned to the door and saw his father still standing there in the distant car park. Toby had thought that was a little unusual and he frowned. He paused for a moment but then entered the classroom and was lost from his father's view.

When he could see his son no longer Toby's father climbed back into his car and drove away slowly. Then, later on that day, he made himself disappear.

Toby was very upset at the time and I knew that his father was never very far away from his thoughts. After it happened we didn't talk very much about his father disappearing himself. I knew, however, that Toby missed him terribly and was still waiting for him to come back.

Chapter 6

First Strike

Following the successful test of Theo's latest invention it was agreed that we should plan and undertake a mission to deploy the fabulous fruit flinger against our common enemy – Wayne Galbraith and his idiotic football-playing friends. The decision to move against them immediately was not taken lightly. Indeed, it was only agreed to after much discussion and after a number of alternative, softer targets had been put forward for further testing and then discarded.

Theo's sister Filomena had been the obvious first choice. However, after the exploding mobile phone affair and the hands-free toilet paper debacle Theo thought it might be better to steer clear of her for a while. For safety reasons.

Leroy suggested that we go after the Creigh twins, who were two loud and rather spiteful girls in our class. Most of the girls – and all of the boys – were scared of them and they ruled the classroom activity corner with two pairs of iron fists.

The Creigh twins were a definite possibility for an additional test but it was thought that they might be too difficult to pin down. Outside of school they were only ever seen riding around on their BMX bikes and they were always together. It might be possible to get them to stop for long enough to get off a clear fling but our chances were slim and the likelihood of a successful escape on foot was virtually nil. The thought of being ridden down and savaged by the enraged Creigh twins was too horrible to contemplate. So they were set aside as well.

It was Toby who finally brought things to a head. "Forget about all this dithering and further testing," he said emphatically. "We know that the fabulous fruit flinger works. Look what it did to my skivvy. My mother went mental. She was all set to come over and give Theo's mum a belting."

"So what happened?" asked Leroy.

"Yes," said Theo, who was intrigued by the possibility of Toby's mother wreaking havoc on the Thorne household. "What happened? Why didn't she?"

Toby shrugged. "She realised she was out of ciggies and decided to go to the shops instead."

"Just as well," said Theo. "My mother would have ripped your mum's head off."

"I don't think so," replied Toby, with a sarcastic laugh. "When my mother gets annoyed she can take anyone apart. Once she got stuck into that big beefy butcher near the pharmacy about some iffy sausages he gave her and she made him cry. Look, the flinger works a treat. We know it does. So let's just go for it. Let's get Galbraith and his slimy mates."

The rest of us looked at each other uncertainly but the die was cast. The decision had been made. It was to be Wayne Galbraith and his band of pesky pinhead pals and there was to be no going back. This was it.

We started planning. An operation like this, after all, required a lot of very careful planning. Theo and I always liked this part, but Toby and Leroy tended to get a bit impatient. If it was left to them we'd have the flinger loaded and ready and would be scouring the streets for Galbraith straight away. Theo was the ideas man, however, and therefore the unproclaimed leader of our band, so everyone fell in line behind him and did what he suggested.

Although Wayne Galbraith was our primary target, we didn't want to tackle him straight away. Leroy, ever the military strategist, thought that it would be good to make our prey sweat a little by picking off his friends first and then drawing the noose in tighter and tighter around him. Let the fear build slowly, went Leroy's diabolically clever argument, so that he knows that it's coming but he doesn't know where or when.

One Sunday afternoon we drew up the list and the order in which the attacks would take place. Here is a copy of that list:

1. Gregor Scoulidis (Scabby)

2. Paul Viner (Whiner)

3. Alex Zaffino (Alphabet)

4. Terry Staton (Stinks)

5. Wayne Galbraith (Bonehead)

The above list, as you can see, includes the nicknames that each of the subjects possess. We agreed to use their nicknames as our code names, but as we didn't think Wayne Galbraith had a nickname we decided to use 'Bonehead' for him.

Theo thought that we should use their code names instead of their real names whenever we discussed the mission. Just in case anyone should overhear us, get wind of what we were doing, and try to warn our targets. Theo went on to suggest that the main threats to our plans were probably our own families, so we had to keep them in the dark as much as possible.

Leroy piped up at this point and said that if our parents suspected that we were up to something they might try to torture the details out of us. What should we do then?

Theo thought the chance of that happening was probably quite slim. If it did, however, it was up to the operative concerned to withstand any pressure and pain that was applied for as long as they possibly could. If one of us was taken and tortured, by our parents or by anybody else, we needed to keep our mouths shut for as long as we could to give the other members of the group a chance to complete the mission.

The strategy we adopted was simple. Theo, as inventor of the weapon and chief technical expert, would have a dual role. He would look after the fabulous fruit flinger and ensure that it was in tip-top condition mechanically. As the most practiced in its use he would also have responsibility for its actual deployment. In other words, he would be the one throwing the tomato at the target.

Leroy, quick with his hands and familiar with all sorts of

weapons, both real and imagined, would serve as our ammunition supremo. He would load and prime the tomato and pass it to Theo. As Theo's right hand man and deputy it was also Leroy's job to step forward and take Theo's place if Theo should stumble, take a hit, or crack under pressure.

Toby's task was to act as a decoy and to distract the target and whoever else was nearby by whatever means possible. This would allow Leroy and Theo to launch the projectile without interference and then make a quick retreat to safety.

My role was to act as lookout, observer and chronicler. I would watch the overall proceedings, keep an eye out for authority figures or any other unfriendlies and film the event using Theo's miniature video camera.

The mission, we decided, would commence on the following morning. We would try to target one subject per day and conclude the operation with a Friday attack on Wayne Galbraith.

Having agreed on the broad strategy we spent the rest of the afternoon ironing out the final details and lounging around on the seats in Mrs Thorne's open-topped Maserati. There was lots of laughter and mucking about but underneath the frivolity I could sense the tension building inexorably. The following day could not come quickly enough.

When Gregor Scoulidis dressed for school on Monday morning he had no idea what lay in store for him. A slim and rather sickly boy, he seemed prone to mishap and was often fronting up to school with band-aids on his face or his arm in a sling or something. His parents were close friends with Mr and Mrs Galbraith and as a result the two boys had grown up together.

Personally, I didn't think that Gregor was too bad by himself, away from Galbraith, but when I said so Toby and Leroy were unswerving in their denunciations.

"If Scabby chooses to hang around with someone like Galbraith then he deserves what's coming to him," was Leroy's view. Toby was in full agreement, and so, it must be said, was Theo.

I must say that this attitude surprised me a little, coming from Theo. I suspected, however, that the identity of the subject was really not all that important to Theo. He was simply interested in seeing the effects of his latest invention on a live, unsuspecting recipient. To him, it didn't really matter who the target was. What mattered most were the efficiency, effectiveness and impact of his work.

That morning Toby, Theo and I met up with Leroy at his house and from there we walked to school. Our topic of discussion: when would be the best time to strike.

Theo and I thought that after school might be a good time to strike and it would allow us the best chance of escape. Toby and Leroy, however, thought that before school began would be better. That way, if the strike was successful, Gregor would have to remain in that tomato-spattered state for the whole school day. Furthermore, the aftermath of the assault would be right under Galbraith's nose for hours on end, as Gregor sat opposite him in class.

The fear would begin to build.

Theo and I had to admit that this had a certain appeal. So we agreed to aim for a strike on or before the school's morning siren. If that proved impossible then we would take our opportunity whenever it next arose throughout the course of the day.

We were confident that we could pull the mission off. But there were risks as well and it was impossible to plan for every eventuality. We didn't know what would happen. We couldn't predict the future. Nobody could predict the future, not even Toby's dad.

As it happened, though, it was easier than any of us expected. It was all so very easy.

We arrived at school about fifteen minutes before classes began. A quick scan of the grounds and the schoolbags lined up outside our classroom revealed that Gregor had not yet arrived.

We moved back towards the school's main entrance, took up our positions and waited.

The seconds ticked by. Toby was waiting not far from the main gate. A stream of kids were coming through that gate and making their way up the path. Theo and Leroy stood on the grass just off the path leading from the gate to the classrooms. I stood off to the other side, a short distance away, with a clear view of the gate, the path and the classrooms.

A bus pulled up and disgorged a mass of noisy children. I could feel the tension building within me. Theo stood very still, his schoolbag on the ground near his feet, a small paper bag in his left hand. Leroy was hopping from foot to foot and Toby was leaning on the fence watching the approaching cars. He was eating a packet of crisps.

We exchanged the odd greeting with kids that we knew as they walked past.

More seconds ticked by. More kids arrived and walked

up the path. The seconds became minutes.

Still no sign of Gregor.

Where was he? Was he sick? Would he be absent today? The siren would be sounding at any moment. A drop of sweat rolled uncomfortably from my armpit all the way down my side and into the waistband of my shorts.

The stream of arriving pupils had slowed to a trickle. We saw Alex Zaffino walk through the gate. He was by himself and we could have taken him instead of Gregor if we had wanted to. But we held our heads and remained in our positions. We had a plan and we needed to stick to it.

We may have been nervous and inexperienced at this kind of guerilla warfare but self-discipline was important and at that moment our self-discipline was tremendous. So we held back and let one of our enemies – the Alphabet – walk through our trap unimpeded.

There was still no sign of Gregor, though. Maybe he wasn't coming to school today. Or maybe he had slipped through our deadly net unseen. Maybe he had a dental appointment or something and was coming to school later. Maybe we should have hit the Alphabet hard when we had the chance.

I was just about to call for the attack to be aborted when I saw Gregor arrive. His parent's black Mercedes cruised slowly up the driveway then stopped just outside the gate. The front window rolled down and a moustachioed face looked out and towards the school. That must be his dad, I thought. The last time I saw his mother she had very little facial hair. It looked as though the face was staring directly at me. I felt very conspicuous standing there with my schoolbag in one hand and a video camera in the other.

Gregor emerged from the back door of the car and said something through the window to the driver. Then he walked to, and then through, the gate. The black Mercedes lurched forward and drove slowly off.

The mission was on.

My nerves were suddenly on edge and my heart started thumping so loudly in my chest that I looked around to see if anybody else could hear it.

Gregor was walking by himself with his bag slung over his left shoulder. His shirt was neatly ironed and very clean. There was nobody close to him. Theo would have a clear shot. Leroy's hops increased their pace and intensity. I knew exactly what he was thinking. It was this: what are you waiting for?

Leroy was awaiting my signal. He was waiting for the attack to commence. He wanted me to act.

I took a deep breath and scanned the entire area a final time. Observing no immediate threat, I switched on the video camera and gave them the piercing whistle they were waiting for.

Oh dear.

I'm not very good at whistling, I have to admit. I should have done some practice or brought a bottle and blown across the top.

My whistle was pathetic.

It sounded like nothing more than a moist puff of air. How embarrassing. But either it was just loud enough for the others to hear or they saw my lips purse and that was enough. They sprang into action.

Theo pulled the pre-cut tomato out of the bag and gave it to Leroy. Theo then pulled the fabulous fruit flinger out of the bag and primed it. Leroy took it from him and stuffed it into the tomato. He made sure that pulp covered the flinger and filled its cup and then gave it back.

So far, so good.

While this was happening Toby theatrically trundled up towards Gregor. When he was alongside him he suddenly gave a great shout and fell over most dramatically. His schoolbag went flying and his crisps scattered all over the damp grass.

It was, I have to admit, a spectacular diversion and it was quite wonderful to behold. Toby had excelled. Had I not been busy with other tasks I would have applauded.

From my vantage point I could see that the majority of the crisps in Toby's packet had been trapped there by his hand, so that only a subset was ejected when he fell. Toby wasn't stupid. But the effect was still startling and dramatic.

Gregor stopped dead and stared at Toby lying there sprawled on the turf. Then Theo took two paces forwards, called "Gregor!" and lobbed the tomato.

Now there was no turning back.

Gregor's immediate reaction was to drop his schoolbag and try to catch the projectile heading his way. When it fell short he just looked at it, confused.

The tomato lay on the path directly in front of him, leaking a bit of pulp onto the concrete. Toby stopped exclaiming and thrashing about and watched Gregor from where he lay awkwardly on the grass. Then all of a sudden, with rotten timing, the school siren sounded announcing the commencement of classes. Still looking at the tomato, Gregor reached down and picked up his bag.

We were going to lose him, I realised. We were going to

crash and burn. We were going to fail on our first real mission.

Then Leroy sprang into action. Taking a quick step forward he screamed: "Gregor, don't move!"

Gregor froze and as he did so the fabulous fruit flinger went off. The tomato give a little jump and a red stain appeared on Gregor's crisp blue shirt, just above the navel. Gregor looked down at it and appeared lost and confused. He dropped to his knees.

"What the . . . ?" muttered Gregor to himself.

At this point Toby scrambled to his feet, collecting the tomato and the fabulous fruit flinger in the process. Then we all raced off to class leaving Gregor kneeling on the path by himself.

I glanced over my shoulder as we ran. It was a pitiful sight. Gregor was motionless and still on his knees. His hands were clutching at his stomach, and red tomato juice was oozing through his fingers.

We had succeeded. We were triumphant. As we jogged to our class I couldn't help but feel, however, a little sorry for Gregor. He had looked so befuddled and pathetic.

A few minutes later Gregor entered the class. The lower part of his shirt was still damp from the scrubbing he had given it but the stain was clearly visible. Mr Cranston laughed and stopped combing his moustache with an old toothbrush when he saw him.

"What happened to you, Scoudoolis?"

"It's Scoulidis, sir. And nothing happened, sir."

"Did you chunder on yourself again?"

"No, sir."

"Throw your breakfast down your shirt?"

"No, sir. It's just a bit of muck, sir."

"All right then, Gregor. Fun's over, sit down."

Gregor took his place and pulled his books and pens out of his desk. As he did so he looked over and gave us all a filthy look.

"One down," whispered Leroy, "and four to go."

"Shut up, Mini-moy, you cloth-eared berk."

"Yes, sir. Sorry, sir."

We stayed well away from Gregor, Wayne Galbraith and his other friends for the rest of the day and the following morning we managed to get Paul Viner – Whiner – using exactly the same routine.

We had been expecting wariness or suspicion from Whiner but he seemed oblivious to what we were doing. Either Gregor was still confused over exactly what had happened to him the previous day or he hadn't explained it all properly to this friends.

Whatever the case, Whiner was taken by just as much surprise as Gregor had been. It was another brilliantly successful sortie.

Unfortunately for Whiner, however, the projectile caught him on the front of his shorts instead of his shirt. So it wasn't as visible as Gregor's had been. Whiner didn't even notice it, in fact, until some time later when Melanie Arnott sat next to him in class and said, "Oh, gross ... what on earth is THAT?" so loudly that the whole of the class could hear.

The look on Whiner's face was priceless. The whole class started giggling and Mr Cranston laughed so hard that a button flew off his shirt. His laughter then transmogrified into a bout of coughing so bad and prolonged that he had to remove himself to the staff toilet for the next fifteen or twenty minutes. Whiner was not impressed but we were all jubilant.

After the Whiner attack Wayne Galbraith and his chums were aware that something was going on. They were highly suspicious and kept on guard. That made things more difficult for us but we were determined to see the mission through.

We tried and failed to get Alex Zaffino on Wednesday before school but we managed to get him at lunchtime when he was coming out of the toilets. The wad of tomato caught him square in his right eye. He yelled in horror and clawed at his face while peering up in all directions at the sky with his remaining operational eye. Obviously he thought the pulp had fallen on him from above.

Thinking fast and seizing the opportunity, Theo shouted "Yuk, bird poo attack!"

Everyone in earshot yelped and scattered and poor Alex Zaffino howeled and ran back into the toilets, retching horribly. When he emerged his face was pale and his eyes were red. We had all removed ourselves from the scene and rolled around on the grass laughing uncontrollably.

Three days had passed with three outstanding results. Could our successful run continue? As a team we were now working like a well-oiled machine. We knew what we were doing and despite the incredible pressure we could perform our roles smoothly and discreetly.

On Thursday our target was Terry Staton, or 'Stinks' to his close friends. Things were getting much more difficult now. Wayne Galbraith and his cronies were on full alert and were very jumpy, particularly those who had not yet been attacked. They knew they were being targeted and they had a fair idea that we were the perpetrators, but they were still unsure about exactly what was happening to them and why.

With this in mind the four of us felt that a new strategy of attack was required. Our opponents were banding together before and after school and also during recess and lunch. It was probably only a matter of time before one of us was approached and queried by one or all of them about what had been going on. After hurried and whispered classroom discussions, then, we decided to hit Stinks on our way to the gymnasium for sport.

Our class had sport every Thursday after lunch. We would make our way from our classroom to the gymnasium and there get changed into our sports clothes. We carried our sports clothes in a bag. This would make it easy for Theo to conceal the fabulous fruit flinger and the requisite tomato.

When it was time for sport Theo and Leroy made sure that they were among the first out of our classroom door. It was no more than a hundred metres from our class to the gymnasium so things had to move fast. Theo was going to launch the flinger whenever he got the chance. He would place it where he could, cross his fingers and hope for the best.

The only real opportunity came when the class arrived at the gymnasium and lined up outside waiting for the command from the teachers to get changed. Theo and Leroy had arrived first and had the tomato primed and ready to go. It was like a time bomb about to go off. It was all set to explode.

The rest of the class shuffled slowly and noisily into position. I could see the tomato concealed in Theo's hands. Both Leroy and Theo looked pale and I could see they were counting down the approximate number of seconds that remained until the flinger went off. If Theo didn't lose it fast the thing would blow up in his hands.

The class settled down and our sports teachers, Mr Frame and Mrs Lewington, came out of the gym. Mr Frame glanced nastily at Theo and Leroy who were still standing separately from the rest of us.

Mr Frame was a bulky man with a crew-cut and he used to be a physical trainer in the air force. When he wasn't taking a class for sport he could usually be found in the gymnasium's weights room pumping iron or doing hundreds of press-ups.

"Line up you two and be quick about it."

"Yes, sir," replied Leroy and Theo in unison. As they moved to fall in with the class Theo let the tomato drop out of his hand. It landed on the ground more or less in line with Stinks but a couple of metres in front of his feet. It was now in plain view, but just behind and to the side of Mrs Lewington.

Several of the children saw the tomato fall and looked to be about to say something. At that moment, though, Mr Frame clapped his hands and called for silence.

"Right class," he began, but before he could go any further the flinger went off. The tomato jumped and a chunk of its pulp went hurtling towards Stinks. The angle wasn't quite right though and the pulp failed to score a direct hit. It scraped along the side of Stinks' neck and ricocheted off his earlobe, disintegrating as it did so. Its remnants careered through the air and spattered onto the two girls standing beside him.

When he felt the pulp hit his neck Stinks gasped and clutched at his throat in shock. "I'm hit," he gurgled horribly. Then he fell backwards into a group of his classmates, dragging several into the ground with him. The two girls to his left, Charlene and Damilola, screamed in terror and ran away, pawing at the sticky gore on their skin and clothing.

At this the rest of the class scattered in all directions, yelling, and so did Mr Frame and Mrs Lewington. Mr Frame shouted something unintelligible and bolted back into the gymnasium as fast as he could, shouldering aside several children as he did so. He slammed the gymnasium's heavy door behind him, right in Mrs Lewington's face. Disoriented by the door to her face and with nowhere to go she panicked, setting off at high speed across the oval.

The four of us stood together and watched with great amusement as Mrs Lewington took flight, her long blonde curls streaming behind her. Maintaining an impressive turn of speed she reached the edge of the school grounds, smoothly hurdled the wire perimeter fence and carried on running. Then she vanished from sight among the trees by the river.

Wow.

Except for Stinks and the children cowering on the ground everyone else had gone. Two teachers and most of the class had vanished within the space of fifteen seconds. Theo retrieved the fabulous fruit flinger and put it back in his bag.

"Looks like sport's been cancelled," said Toby.

"Looks like it," agreed Theo.

"Hooray," said Leroy.

It had been a great afternoon.

After the Stinks triumph, the Friday attack on Wayne Galbraith was something of an anti-climax. We managed to get him as he walked out of the classroom at the end of the day. He had been vigilant all morning and afternoon but with the final siren he let down his guard for a moment. That was all we required. Theo had the fabulous fruit flinger set up outside the classroom door and timed Galbraith's approach by watching him through the window.

Two seconds after coming through the door Wayne Galbraith had a large red stain in the middle of his chest. Mission accomplished.

Despite his earlier watchfulness I think that by Friday afternoon Wayne had resigned himself to the inevitable. His reaction was pathetic. He simply looked down at his chest then up at Leroy and me. We had our bags in our hands and were ready to flee. Theo had already grabbed the spent tomato and scarpered. Toby was nowhere to be seen. Maybe he had pulled his father's disappearing trick.

Expecting fireworks from Galbraith Leroy and I were surprised when nothing happened. He looked at us a moment longer, his eyes giving nothing away. Then he simply turned away and slowly walked over to where his bag was hanging on the rail.

Chapter 7

The Celebration

As Leroy and I walked back to his house I was surprised to find myself feeling rather flat, although I couldn't explain why. Leroy, however, was jubilant and very talkative. He felt that the mission had run so smoothly that we should do it all over again the following week. Maybe with some different targets though.

I wasn't so sure about that so I just mumbled something neutral in reply. The mission had been a resounding success, it was true, but I didn't feel as triumphant as I expected to.

When we met up again with Theo and Toby at Leroy's house I was relieved to hear that the two of them sided with me.

"We did it," said Theo, "and we did it well. But I don't think there's any point in doing it all again. It wouldn't be as good. We'd probably be disappointed. I think it's time to move on." Theo had never been one to rest on his laurels.

"Yes," agreed Toby. "Let's do something else. We don't

want to get Galbraith and the rest of them too riled up."

"We can celebrate our victory, though," said Theo. "We deserve it after all the effort we put in and the way things worked out. It was brilliant. It all worked like clockwork. I'll tell you what, how about a barbecue at my place tomorrow? Come on over. Have lunch with us. You're all invited."

"What was that?" asked Leroy, who had been distracted by a motorbike going by. "Are you going to throw a barbecue?"

"Don't be daft. I'm not doing a barbecue but my parents are having one. Loads of people will be there. I'm sure they won't mind if you three come. They probably won't even notice. Come along, we'll have some fun."

"Count me in," said Toby, who was always up for a feed, especially if it was at someone else's place and he liked the sound of what was on offer.

"Me too," I said.

"Okay," said Leroy. "Maybe we could deploy the fabulous fruit flinger at the barbecue, then. We could easily get a stack of people there. Grown-ups or other kids."

"No," said Theo. "The flinger should probably go into storage for a while. It needs to be degreased, documented and catalogued. We'll do something else at the barbecue."

"Righto."

"See you all tomorrow, then."

"See you."

Shortly after noon on the following day, then, Toby rode his bike the very short distance to my house. Initially he was going to walk over, but mindful of the fact that during the past school week we had assaulted five different boys with tomatoes, all of whom probably lived in the neighbourhood, he thought it prudent to give himself a speedier form of transportation. Just in case a quick getaway from somewhere should be required.

This was sensible thinking – unusual for Toby – so I pulled my bike out of the garage, brushed a few cobwebs off and pumped up the back tyre. Toby waited as I did so, practicing some rather lame bunny hops over the curb. When I was satisfied with the state of my tyres we rode to Theo's house together.

There were at least fifteen cars parked in the street outside Theo's house and several on the driveway. It looked to be quite a large affair, which was most unlike the barbecues we had at my house. Those were usually attended by my immediate family and perhaps, on occasion, one or two other people at most.

Theo's house, though, was buzzing with noise and activity. As Toby and I climbed off our bikes I half expected a uniformed valet to emerge from the garage to park them for us. I waited for a moment but no valet appeared, uniformed or otherwise, so I leant my bike next to Toby's against the front wall of the house. Then we walked up the steps to the front door.

Filomena saw us arrive from a window and opened the door before we even had a chance to knock. She gave me a dirty look and then turned to Toby and gave him a *very* dirty look. For a moment it looked as though Filomena was going to let Toby have it in some way and I could feel him tense beside me in readiness for an intense verbal or physical assault. After an awkward pause, though, she bit her lip and simply said that Theo and his creepy pal were upstairs in Theo's bedroom.

Filomena stood aside to let us pass. As she did Toby started fumbling in his pocket. I started to get a strong sense of foreboding.

"Hey Filomena," said Toby. "Have a look at this."

I nearly tripped over the threshold in disbelief.

What was Toby doing?

This was a most unexpected development. Toby was playing with fire with this girl. After the hands-free toilet paper debacle Toby should have been keeping as much distance as was humanly possible between him and Filomena. He knew what she was capable of. We all did. I took a further step away from them and felt my heart rate accelerate.

Toby found whatever it was he'd been searching for in his pocket and yanked his hand out. I don't know what I expected and from the look on her face Filomena obviously felt the same way. A frog, a severed finger, a handkerchief with a giant bogey – with Toby it could have been anything.

Thankfully, it was none of those things. It was nothing ghastly at all. In Toby's hand was a small plastic object about the length of his little finger. It was shaped like a miniature shovel or a canoeist's paddle, with a wide flat end to look at and a narrow strip to hold. On the flat end was a single red dot.

"Watch carefully," said Toby, holding the object low in front of Filomena. Mistrustful but intrigued she bent forward slightly, her eyes locked on his hand. Toby started humming and his other hand began tracing a mysterious pattern under, over and around the plastic paddle. This went on for some time, with Toby's humming gradually getting louder.

"Keep watching . . . keep watching," Toby murmured, then resumed humming. After a few more seconds Toby broke the spell with a loud "HUTT!" and before our eyes the single red dot had miraculously become two.

"*Yes!*" exclaimed Toby.

Filomena was not so thrilled. "That was pretty pathetic," she said. "Is that the best you can do?" She gave him another dirty look then closed the front door and went back into her father's study, shutting the door behind her. Toby stared for a moment at the closed door.

"Not bad, Toby," I said as we walked upstairs. "I thought that was pretty good, actually."

"Pretty good?" repeated Toby. "That wasn't pretty good, it was a triumph."

I thought that was a bit of a stretch. "It was okay, but I don't think I'd call it a triumph. It went on too long, with all that humming and everything."

At that Toby sniggered. "Ah, but I needed all that humming. I needed it to drag on." He held his hand up with his index finger about a centimetre away from his thumb. "I was that close to Filomena. I could smell her. I had to make it last. I was almost touching her. I drew her in. A bit longer and I could have commenced the hypnosis. That will happen next time. I've drawn her in once now and next time she won't be so wary. So it wasn't just pretty good, it was a triumph. It was magic, pure magic."

"What?" I said, unable to keep the disgust – and maybe a bit of envy – out of my voice. "Why do you want to smell her? Why do you want to hypnotise her? And if you want to touch her why don't you just insult her or remind her of your toilet caper – she's bound to give you a Chinese burn."

"Why should I give her the upper hand?" Toby responded. "I want the upper hand with that one, and . . ."

Toby stopped talking as we entered Theo's bedroom. Theo's room was probably twice the size of my bedroom at home. Aside from his bed and the usual furniture and clothes the room was full of scientific, electrical and mechanical tools and equipment. Books and posters lined the walls and model spacecraft were suspended on thin wires from the ceiling.

Theo and Leroy were sitting on the floor tinkering with a robotic gnome that Theo had built some months earlier. It resembled your average garden gnome, of the type available in most garden centres and plant nurseries. Theo hoped to slip it one night into the garden of his neighbour, Mrs Cartwright.

Aside from martial arts and storming through houses looking for burglars Mrs Cartwright was keen on roses, fresh vegetables and garden furniture. She also had a number of gnomes scattered around her property. Theo had purchased a similar gnome but had filled its hollow core with silicon chips and speakers and added four concealed robotic legs to its base. All of us, and especially Theo, thought that it was another masterpiece.

When working properly Theo's robotic gnome would, upon receiving the signal from the transmitter on Theo's side of the fence, unfold its legs and rise about a foot off the ground. It would then start lurching forward screeching *"DIE, DIE, DIE!"*

Theo thought that this would be pretty hilarious to see and so did we. But he was having a bit of trouble getting the robotic legs working the way that he wanted them to.

When he saw us come in Theo set his gnome aside, crawled across to his window and peered outside. "Food's on," he said. Then he stood up, grasped Leroy's hand and pulled him to his feet.

"Are you hungry?" asked Theo. I nodded, and so did Toby.

"I'm starving," said Leroy.

"Let's go then."

Theo's back garden was much larger than ours and even so it was full of activity. There were people everywhere. Most of them were adults, of course, but there was also a scattering of other children, the majority of whom seemed younger than us.

"Gee, your parents sure know a whole bunch of people," Toby remarked, surveying the scene.

"They do," said Theo, leading us over to where the food was being dished out. He clapped his hands with relish and said, "Get stuck in, gang."

This was unlike any barbecue that I had been to before. Music was coming from somewhere and all of the guests were dressed quite smartly. There was a long table covered in a white cloth piled high with breads, cheese, finger foods and salad. A pretty young woman in a white uniform was overseeing the table and helping guests with their servings. Behind her stood a huge wood-fired hot-plate on wheels, laden with meat, seafood and sausages. It was being tended by a massive dark-skinned man wearing whites and a tall chef's hat. And when I say massive I mean massive in the muscular sense, not massively fat.

Mrs Thorne was standing next to the huge chef, holding a glass of champagne daintily in one hand and pointing at something on the hot-plate with the other. The chef waved his tongs airily and said something to her in a deep rumble. I couldn't make out what he had said, but Mrs Thorne slapped him on the shoulder, threw her elegantly coiffured head back and laughed. She certainly seemed to be enjoying herself.

The four of us grabbed a plate each and worked our way along the table, loading it up. A sausage in a bun appeared to be the order of the day, for us at least, with Toby going for two. Plenty of onions and tomato sauce, which had us all giggling.

"Don't get it on your shirt or pants, now," said Theo, and the rest of us cracked up.

After we filled our plates Theo led us over to the makeshift bar which had been erected next to the gazebo. It was manned by a young fellow who was also clad head-to-toe in white. I could see where the music was coming from now. On the gazebo a string quartet was playing some boring classical music piece, and a toddler in a floral dress with muck on her face was bouncing up and down in front of them.

"So what'll it be, folks?" asked the barman. He had an open bottle of vodka in one hand and an ice scoop in the other. Rows of bottles stood on the temporary shelves behind him and he was surrounded by portable glass-topped refrigerators. Theo stepped forward.

"I'll have a whiskey and soda, please," said Theo. The young man behind the bar put down his ice scoop.

"Ho ho ho," he went, but it wasn't really a laugh. It was more like some kind of nasty sarcastic remark.

"Make mine a scotch on the rocks, no ice," said Toby.

"Ho ho double beeping ho," said the bartender. "You guys are real comedians. Stop it, you're killing me. I can't take it anymore."

"Oh, yeah," said Toby.

"All right, that's enough. Now what do you midgets want? And hurry it up, too. I've got real people to serve."

"In that case," said Theo, "I'll just have a glass of your finest lemonade."

"Here you go mate, you can have a whole can. I'm nothing if not generous. What do the rest of you imbeciles want? Hurry up, or you'll get a thump instead of a drink."

"Same as him," said Leroy.

"Same as him," repeated Toby.

"Lemonade, please," I said.

With our food in one hand and our drinks in the other we escaped the drinks zone and wandered around the garden trying to settle on somewhere to sit and eat. Toby wondered aloud where Filomena might be but Theo told him not to worry about her.

"You know she's still mad about that incident in the toilet. If I was you I'd keep right away from her. Otherwise you might find something in your food that you'd prefer not to eat."

We walked towards the back of the garden where a number of hired plastic chairs sat empty. Then Theo noticed his father there, hemmed into the corner by Mrs Cartwright and another fearsome looking woman. That could only be one of Mrs Cartwright's security guard chums, I thought.

Theo's father appeared very uncomfortable with his situation. He looked as though he would prefer to be somewhere else in the garden but the two women seemed to be having a great time. Mrs Cartwright was holding a sausage in her hand and saying something and the other woman was laughing fit to burst. The noise of her loud cackles and snorts carried easily across the busy garden, drowning out both the music and the sounds of conversation around us.

At that moment Mr Thorne caught sight of his son and his face lit up in relief. He hopped once or twice on the spot and urgently waved Theo over. Theo pretended not to see his father and quickly turned on his heel. We started walking back towards the house.

Weaving our way through the groups of people eating, drinking and talking became more difficult the closer we got to the house. In addition to the many guests there was also more furniture and catering equipment to dodge. We needed to find somewhere to sit, and fast. Otherwise one or more of us was going to have some mishap with our food or drink.

I was following Leroy through a press of people when all of a sudden and without warning he stopped abruptly. I banged into his back and the force of the collision almost sent my hot dog flying into the lap of an elderly woman wearing pearls and a blue dress.

"Holy cow!" exclaimed Leroy. "Is that Whiner?"

I looked in the direction he was nodding.

Well, fancy that. It was Whiner. What was he doing here?

Whiner, also known as Paul Viner, was standing near the shallow end of the swimming pool. He was tucking into what appeared, at distance, to be a steak sandwich. As he took a bite I could see what looked like lettuce, cheese and onions starting to slide out the side. Toby appeared next to me. I kept my eyes on Whiner and watched as a chunk of food – a slice of cucumber, perhaps – fell from his sandwich and dropped into the pool.

"What is it?" asked Toby, scanning the crowd.

"It's Whiner," I replied. "Can't you see him? He's over there by the pool eating a steak sandwich."

"It can't be. Are you sure?"

"Well, I think it's a steak sandwich, but I can't be certain, I suppose. But it is Paul Viner." By then Theo had joined us as well and wanted to know what was going on.

Whiner was standing next to a smartly dressed man and woman who looked as though they might be his parents. Whiner hadn't noticed us yet but the man was looking in our direction.

"Blimey," said Theo. "I think Whiner's dad knows my mum. This is terrible. We can't be having this. Let's get out of here."

"Where shall we go?" asked Leroy. "Inside?"

"No, there are people in there already. Let's go in the garage."

Following Theo we slipped through the back entrance of the garage and vaulted over the doors of the open-topped Maserati. Settling onto the luxurious leather seats we started tucking into our hot dogs and congratulated ourselves on the closeness of our escape.

What the heck was Whiner doing here? We couldn't believe it. How could we enjoy ourselves with people like him around?

Thank goodness we had filled our plates prior to spotting him. At least we could hide away in the garage and eat now. There was no real need for us to return to the barbecue. If we needed more food and drink we could probably get it from inside the house.

It was much quieter in the garage and we all enjoyed being away from the press of people outside. Our peace and solitude, however, was not to last very long.

Chapter 8

Maserati Magic

We had been loafing in the garage for less than five minutes when we were startled by a voice close behind us.

"Good grief, Theo, does your mother know what you lot do in here?"

It was the man we had seen outside standing next to Whiner. He had slipped silently through the door behind us and was standing at the rear of the Maserati. He had a beef roll in one hand and a glass of red wine in the other.

We all yelped and twisted around to see him better. Well, three of us yelped. Toby, who was sitting in the back seat right in front of the man, made more of a choking noise and sent a spray of food particles and lemonade onto the back of the driver's seat.

"Stay as you are, stay as you are," the man said. "Don't get excited. And try not to choke, Toby."

The man walked around to the front of the Maserati and we all resumed our positions, facing forwards, hot dogs in hand and sauce dripping everywhere.

Leroy sneaked a bite of his hot dog.

The man was tall, with short dark hair, and he was wearing a dark suit and white shirt without a tie. His face was thin, like Whiner's, and he was wearing steel-rimmed spectacles.

I had always thought that spectacles made someone look like a nerd but there was nothing nerdish about this man. Nothing at all. He just looked lean and tough. Perhaps it hadn't been such a good idea to have a go at Whiner.

"Don't worry, Theo," said the man, who must surely have been Whiner's dad. He had a soft, faintly menacing voice. "Don't worry, I won't tell your mother. It can be our little secret, yes?"

Theo, in the driver's seat, nodded blankly. Then he said, "How do you know who we are? Are you Whi – Paul's dad?"

"I am Paul's father, yes. You can call me Mr Viner."

Mr Viner stopped talking for a moment and let his hard stare settle on each of us in turn. He took a sip of his wine, followed by a bite of his roll.

"How do I know who you are? Well, I know all about each one of you. I know lots of things. You'd probably be surprised at how much I do know. Some of what I know has come from the school, some has come from Paul, and some has come from, shall we say, other sources."

Other sources? What did that mean? That sounded ominous. I didn't like the sound of that. I slipped a little further down into my seat.

The man looked at Leroy and frowned. "Hello Leroy. I know all about you, young man, you and your father. You have a lovely mother, though."

Leroy just sat there, gaping at the man like a fish on its way out.

Mr Viner then turned his attention to me. "What are you doing in here with these three?" he asked.

What did that mean? Shouldn't I have been in here with Theo, Leroy and Toby? Did Whiner's dad think that I should have been somewhere else? What *was* he going on about?

I returned Mr Viner's look but I didn't say anything, so he carried on talking.

"I know all about you, too. More than you might think. I know about Westlake Primary, for instance, and what happened there before you left."

Westlake Primary was the school I attended prior to starting at Hampton last year. I didn't think that anyone, apart from my parents, knew about Westlake. Not in this town anyway. I was starting to feel very uneasy.

"What happened at Westlake Primary?" asked Theo, putting his hand up automatically. Trust Theo to be a nosy parker.

"Nothing that need concern you," snapped Mr Viner, thankfully. "You mind your own business and don't worry about it. And put your hand down, for goodness sake. You're not in school now."

Mr Viner slowly walked away from the Maserati and half-leaned, half-sat on the bonnet of Mrs Thorne's Porsche. One of his feet stayed on the floor and the other was raised, his knee pointing at Leroy. His heel drummed slowly against the tyre. I sat there looking at the back of Leroy's head. I could see the skin behind his ears flex as he chewed on his hot dog.

"Listen, I know what's been going on at school between you lot and Paul and his friends. Yes. A bit of mild bullying, I hear. Hmm? A bit of pushing and shoving, maybe? A few harsh words, a bit of retaliation, that sort of thing?"

Theo started to defend our actions but Mr Viner cut him off before he could get his first sentence out. He was still speaking softly but his voice, menacing before, now had a nasty edge to it.

"Shut up, Theo. I'm not concerned about all that. It's nothing much. Schoolyard high jinks, I'm sure. But that's not why I'm here. I'm not interested in what you lot do in the playground. I was bullied at school all the time and it didn't hurt me. It toughened me up, probably. Turned me into the man I am today."

Which is what? I couldn't help but ask myself the question. What kind of man was Whiner's dad? Did he think he was some kind of tough guy? Someone who likes hassling young kids at barbecues and making them feel uncomfortable? Or was he some variety of beef-eating wine-drinking psychopath? Maybe he'd tell us what kind of man he was. Maybe not.

Mr Viner took another bite of his roll.

"Mmm, this is delicious. Very tasty. You lot should skip the hot dogs and get a beef roll. Well, maybe not you, Toby."

Well, there's a clue as to the type of man he was. An adult who was not above poking fun at a twelve year old's fondness for food.

"Look, I'm not here to tell you off or to get you in trouble."

"Great," said Toby.

"But I could if I want to," he said.

"Great," said Toby, rather less enthusiastically.

Mr Viner took another sip of his wine and licked his lips. Then, once again, he carefully looked at each of us in turn, taking his time about, too.

None of us said anything. We just sat there, motionless, like four rather small and scruffy crash-test dummies waiting for the Maserati to go smashing into the side of the garage wall. I had the feeling that Mr Viner could have arranged that if he wanted to.

Licking his lips, Mr Viner leaned forward. He looked a bit like the smooth villain in the movies. You know the type. The smart cruel one, not the big stupid one. Just before he plunged his deadly stiletto into someone's guts and gave it a twist.

"Believe it or not but I'm here," he murmured, "to ask for your help."

This was unexpected. I think we were all taken aback. I know I was. Why would someone like Mr Viner be asking for our help? Why us? What could we possibly do that could help him?

I didn't like the sound of this at all. I don't know how many instincts I have but all of them were telling me that when a man like Mr Viner asks for help it's time to bolt. It's time to excuse oneself to the lavatory then squeeze through the window and take off at high speed.

I wanted to take off but I couldn't. I was trapped in a garage. I was trapped on the back seat of a luxurious Maserati. It's not quite the same as having your leg in a wire loop hanging upside down from a tree but it's trapped nonetheless. I felt cornered and helpless.

Maybe all this had something to do with Paul. Maybe Mr Viner wanted us to be friends with his son or something sappy like that.

I didn't think so, however. This guy didn't look like that kind of pansy. If anything, I suspected, he would probably ask us to be tougher on his son, to rough him up good and proper and make a man of him.

"Um, how can we help you?" asked Theo.

I was glad that Theo could still talk. My tongue felt as though it had swollen up to twice its normal size. I could barely breathe, let alone speak.

"Well, before I answer that, let me tell you something about myself," said Mr Viner, taking another sip of his wine and making himself comfortable on the Porsche.

If Mrs Thorne was to enter the garage now and see Mr Viner lounging on the bonnet of her Porsche and her Maserati stuffed with messy children she'd have a fit.

"Not many people know this but I work for the government – mainly in the area of computers, security and stuff. Which, incidentally, is how I came to know your mother, Theo. Now, some of the work I do involves making enquiries about certain events and certain people, which is why I know so much about all of you. You could say that I have access to a lot of information."

"A lot of information," repeated Theo, for some reason known only to himself.

"Yes, a lot of information," confirmed Mr Viner. "Now most of the time I can get all of the information I need by myself but in some cases I need a little bit of help. Maybe from the people who work for me or maybe from people like your mum, Theo. Or your dad, Leroy. Or even, in certain circumstances, from people like you."

"People like us?" asked Toby.

"Yes, Toby, people like you. Sometimes, kid, I need help from people like you. Believe me, it isn't often, thankfully."

"Is that what you want, then?" asked Theo. "You want us to help you to find out about something? I know a lot about science and Leroy is ace on guns and stuff."

"Oh, really? Guns and stuff, you say?"

"Yes, he knows all about them. He's an expert on all types of weaponry."

"Shut up, Theo," said Leroy.

"I'm just saying – "

"Well don't say."

"Yes, shut up, Theo. I don't need to know about guns. Or any other weaponry, for that matter. If I need advice on weapons I don't need to go to a twelve year old for it, I can tell you that now. I know plenty of people who do nothing but mess around with guns all day. No, I'm not after information on a something."

"A someone, then?" asked Toby.

"That's it, big boy, a someone. Exactamundo."

"What?" said Toby.

"Exactamundo."

"Eh?"

"Exactamundo. Isn't that how you kids talk these days? Exactamundo . . . that's gas, man . . . he's nuttin but a froot . . . isn't that the lingo?"

"I don't know what you're talking about."

"Okay, point taken. Anyway, I need information on a someone."

"Who is it?" asked Leroy. "Is it someone at school? It's

112

Mr Dunn, isn't it? I bet you it is. I always knew he was an evil nutter."

Mr Dunn was the principal. I didn't think he was that bad as far as principals go. He might have been a nutter, but he wasn't an evil nutter. Leroy didn't like him because last term he had confiscated his home-made knuckle-dusters.

"No, it wouldn't be Mr Dunn," argued Toby. "If it's anyone it would have to be Mr Simpson. That guy's completely certifiable."

Mr Viner smiled at them both. "No, it's not someone from school. Although thanks for the tip about Dunn. I don't like him either. A bleeding heart leftie from way back, although you never heard that from me. And Simpson's not much better, to be frank. No, at the moment I have no interest in anyone at your school, apart from you four. But I am interested in someone not far from the school, which is why I thought that you might be able to help me. So, are you able to help me?"

"Um, maybe we can help you," said Theo uncertainly.

"Good," said Mr Viner. "Now don't you worry, it's nothing too difficult and it won't take too long."

"What is it?"

"I'll tell you, but first of all you all have to swear that anything I say to you will remain right here in this garage, just between the five of us. All right?"

We responded with an assortment of reluctant nods and grunts. I heard Leroy belch quietly in front of me.

Mr Viner eyeballed us all again. Then he took off his glasses and eyeballed us some more.

"If I find out that any of you have said anything to

anyone else there's going to be big trouble, okay?"

More nods and grunts, but no audible belches this time.

"Right. Here it is then. Now there's a man I know, a Mr Richardson, who lives on the other side of the river. Just across the river from the school, in fact. You've probably seen his house. It's the grey place with the green roof. You know the one?"

Someone must have nodded. Maybe it was Theo. Maybe it was me. I couldn't be sure.

"Good. Now, Mr Richardson isn't a very sociable guy, and he doesn't seem to like people like me. I can't think why. But I'm sure he won't mind you lot. You seem like a likeable bunch. I mean, I like you and I don't like many people."

Great, I thought. He likes us. Now here it comes.

Crunch time.

Mr Viner continued. "I just need you to go over to his house once or twice, take a look around and tell me what you see. I would do it myself but it's a bit tricky for me. My work has all sorts of dumb rules about what I can and can't do and there's lots of annoying paperwork. On top of all that I am really very busy at the moment. So I can't do it. But if you could do me this favour I would really appreciate it."

"That's it?" asked Theo.

"That's it."

"Just go over to his house and take a look around?"

"Yep."

"We could do that," said Leroy, relieved. "That's a piece of cake. No problem. It would be like an adventure, right? Like a deadly mission of some sort."

"That's exactly right," said Mr Viner. "An adventure. A mission. Although maybe not deadly. But you never know, I might get lucky. No, all you need to do is go and check out this fellow's house and garden. Take a look around and see what he does. If he's not there and you want to take a peep inside you can do that as well."

With those final words the piece of cake that this task was supposed to be suddenly took on a sour taste. This was all starting to make me feel very uncomfortable now. Furthermore, Mr Viner was talking very quickly and I wasn't sure that I had fully taken in all that he had said.

"Why do you need us to do it?" I asked. "Why don't you ask Paul or some of his friends?"

Mr Viner gave me a hard look. "I can't use Paul because of where I work. It's too risky for me and it's too risky for him. And the kids he plays with – Alex, Wayne and Stinks – well, I need people I can rely on, people who are smart and trustworthy. Not those goofballs. I need people like you. Think of it as a compliment."

I wasn't taken in by Mr Viner's smarmy flattery and I still didn't understand why it had to be us.

"Why don't you just drive over there yourself and take a look around, or send a cop car?" I asked.

I received another long hard look and Mr Viner was silent for a moment. He put his wine glass onto the Porsche's bonnet and rubbed his face with his hand.

"Okay guys, I'll give it to you straight. I think I can trust you. I think you're on the level. Are you on the level?"

"We're on the level," said Leroy, although I'm pretty certain he had no idea what he was talking about. I mean, I didn't know what being 'on the level' actually meant, and

I'm sure that Leroy, Toby and Theo didn't know either.

"Of course you are," continued Mr Viner. "You're all on the level. Okay, the truth, then. We're a bit worried about this man that I want you to check out. We don't think he's entirely on the straight and narrow. But we don't know much about him and we can't prove anything. So we can't approach him and we can't send a policeman. I'm afraid we still have some silly laws that won't allow that kind of thing. But there's nothing to stop you four from going over there and having a look around. If he's there, you can talk to him. He might be lonely and want a chat. If he's not there you can take a look around his garden and the area around his house. If you're up for a challenge and you think you've got the guts you might try to get inside and take a proper look around. Rest assured, we won't be too far away, so there's nothing to worry about."

"Well, I'm a bit worried," said Toby.

Thank goodness for Toby. I thought it was going to have to be me again and I was getting a bit tired of being on the receiving end of Mr Viner's hard looks. "What if this bloke is some kind of a nut or something?" asked Toby. "It could be dangerous."

"Don't worry, Toby. We don't think he's a nut. We don't think he's done much of anything yet. And as I said, we won't be too far away. There's always someone around watching and listening and we'll have a helicopter or two in the vicinity."

Mr Viner slid off the Porsche and picked up his plate and wine glass.

"Look gang, I'd love to stay and chat but I'm going to have to rejoin the party in a minute. It's like this. Theo, a day or two ago your mother was telling me about your interest in hidden sequences."

Theo straightened up at this. I knew he would. Theo was a sucker for anything to do with hidden sequences. Mr Viner carried on with his explanation.

"There are hidden sequences everywhere. The world's absolutely riddled with them. There are far more than you could possibly imagine. I know, I have something of an interest in them myself. If it's possible for something to have a hidden sequence in it you can be sure it will be there."

"Really?" said Theo.

"Of course."

"Wow."

"Yes, it is pretty wow. I mean, you're an inventor, Theo. If you designed something that was able to have a hidden sequence built in would you include it? Well of course you would. Why wouldn't you? If you design and build payphones you'd be a lunatic not to include a sequence that could give you free phone calls every day for the rest of your life."

"True," said Theo. "But what does all this have to do with Mr … what was his name?"

"Richardson."

"Yeah, Mr Richardson?"

"Well, most people have something that resembles a hidden sequence as well. Not quite the same but not really too dissimilar, when you think about it. You all know that when you press buttons things happen. That's what they're for, right? If you know which buttons to press at the railway station you can get on the trains and ride them for free. If you know which buttons to press on the machine at the multiplex you can get a free movie ticket. Well, it's actually a similar thing with people. Push them a certain way and you'll get some kind of response. Press some of their buttons and something will happen. Press some other buttons and something else will happen. If, for example, I was to leap over Leroy's back fence with a samurai sword then I'm bound to get a knife in my chest or an arrow through my eye. Right, Leroy?"

"You betcha," said Leroy, looking quite chuffed at the analogy.

"Well," continued Mr Viner, "we think the potential is there for something to happen with Mr Richardson. If the right buttons are pressed, that is. We want that something to happen when we're around and we think that you fellows can be the buttons to do it. Do you understand what I'm getting at?"

Of course, none of us had any idea whatsoever what Mr Viner was talking about. It was as though mid-way through the conversation he had started speaking in Spanish or Martian. We hadn't a clue.

I just sat there feeling confused and miserable. Somehow we were being suckered into something big time. The one thing I knew for certain was that nothing good could possibly come of it.

None of us spoke.

"It's time for me to go," said Mr Viner. "Your mama's waiting for me, Theo. Look, it's really simple. Go to Mr Richardson's house after school on Monday and take a look around his garden. If he's there say hello to him. If he's not take a peek through his windows. If he's left his door open take a walk inside. Take note of what you see. On Tuesday morning I'll be dropping Paul at school. You can tell me what you know then. Simple, right? Any imbecile could do it. You guys should have no problem."

It *was* simple, or so it seemed, but that didn't mean I had to like it. And I think the others felt the same way. Mr Viner must have sensed the resistance as well. But that didn't seem to perturb him. He seemed like a pretty cool customer. He pointed the remains of his beef roll at each of us in turn.

"This is an important mission and I'm giving it to you, you, you and you. Don't fret, you can do it, no problem. You *can* do it. And if you do it well then I should be able to score a helicopter ride for each of you. If you do it poorly I'll be disappointed. Very disappointed. So disappointed, Theo, that in your case I'll probably feel obliged to tell your mum all about the feasts you have in her Maserati. I know the rest of your parents as well. And what you've been up to. I know about all that stuff. And I even know about all the stuff that I don't know about. So watch it, and remember that I'm watching you."

That clinched it . . . somehow.

"We'll do it," said Theo. "But how do we know that . . . that what you say . . . ?"

Mr Viner drained his glass, straightened his suit and walked over to the back door. Beyond the door we could hear the muted noise of the party and we could see the shadows of the guests falling against the glass bricks of the wall. Beyond that wall lay some semblance of normality, I thought. A world far removed from whatever the heck it was that was going on in here.

"How do you know?" asked Mr Viner, adjusting his steel-rimmed spectacles.

"Yes. How do we know that what you say about Mr Richardson, and his hidden sequence, and . . . ?"

"Theo, put your hot dog and drink down. *Not* on the upholstery, for goodness sake," said Mr Viner.

Theo did as instructed, putting his plate on his lap and passing his lemonade to Leroy.

"Thank you, Theo. Now press and hold down the car's starter button."

Theo paused for a moment, and then did as he was told.

"With the other hand, press and hold down that little button on the odometer."

Theo pressed it.

"Keep your fingers on those buttons. Now reach down with your foot and push the brake pedal three times. It's the middle one."

Theo slid down and stretched out his leg. He found the brake pedal. He gave it three pumps and on the final one the Maserati's engine roared into life. It sounded deafening in the confines of the garage.

"Switch it off, switch it off!" yelled Leroy.

"How?" shouted Theo, waving his arms around in panic.

"Press the starter button again," said Leroy. Theo pressed it and the engine fell silent. Our panic subsided.

"Wow," said Theo. "I mean, wow! That's incredible!" He turned around. Mr Viner was no longer there. He had gone through the door and rejoined the barbecue.

Expecting Mrs Thorne to burst into the garage at any moment we all leaped out of the Maserati and huddled in the alcove. We stayed there a minute or two, hardly daring to breathe. The door from the garage to the garden stayed closed, though, and we remained undisturbed.

"That is one cool sequence," said Theo, jotting it down on a spare scrap of paper for future reference.

"Yes it is," agreed Leroy. "That is one cool sequence for one cool car. I wonder if it works on other cars. It's so cool. And this is one cool barbecue, Theo. Thanks for inviting us."

"No problem, Leroy."

Leroy suddenly clapped his hands and then punched the air with both fists. "And now, best of all, we're going into action. We have a cool mission to perform."

"Yes, we do have a mission," agreed Theo.

"Cool," said Toby.

I wasn't so sure about that. Lots of things about Mr Viner had troubled me. He knew too much about Theo, Leroy and Toby, for instance, and he knew way too much about me. He hadn't said that much about me but I knew that he knew.

Also, he was far too smooth for my liking. I preferred my adults to be funny or eccentric, like Mr Thorne. Or thick, like our teacher, Mr Cranston. I was wary of the intelligent and ambitious ones. They could be dangerous. They seemed to know far more about kids than they had a right to know. Mr Viner appeared to be one of those types. I didn't like those kinds of adults very much, and I didn't like him at all.

Chapter 9

The Mission

The rest of the weekend seemed to fly by and before I knew it we were sitting in class on Monday afternoon waiting for the siren to go off. As usual the closer the clock got to home time the slower it seemed to go.

I hadn't seen Leroy or Theo on Sunday but Theo told me that he spent most of the day looking for more hidden sequences and researching surveillance methods and equipment. He also tried various internet searches on Mr Richardson and his address but drew a blank apart from a couple of very old real estate listings for the house. So that was a bit of a wasted effort.

Leroy laughed when he heard that and said that Theo should ease off on the learning and start priming his puny body for action. Leroy, for example, had spent Sunday practicing his kung fu and his knife throwing.

According to Leroy he had become quite adept at throwing his knife. He had pinned a card to the trunk of a large tree in his back garden and spent hours slinging his knife at it. I had watched him doing this a number of times and on all of those occasions the knife tended to hit the tree handle first then drop to the ground or just bounce off in some other direction. I had yet to see him stick it into the card, or even the tree, point first. I thought that it was a very stupid thing to be doing anyway, not to mention dangerous.

Theo was a bit miffed about the crack about his puny body, and even more so as it had come from Leroy, who despite all of his grandiose talk of weapons and action and fighting was one of the smallest kids in our class. Sometimes Leroy can be quite irritating.

Theo pursed his lips and frowned at Leroy for a moment and looked to be about to say something. Then his gaze shifted towards the window. His eyes widened, he gasped and then he raised his arm to point at something outside. When Leroy turned his head to look in that direction Theo gave him a hard thump on his shoulder with a wicked twist of his knuckles to round it off. Leroy jumped in surprise and nearly fell off his chair.

"Hey," said Leroy, "that hurt. What was that for?"

"Didn't see that one coming, did you?"

"You're a real jerk."

"Got you good, that time."

"Do that again and I'll bust your head," said Leroy.

"You need to sharpen up those reactions a bit, you little squirt," laughed Theo.

"You need to clear off out of my face."

I did see Toby on Sunday, but only for a brief moment. I was sitting on our front steps drawing a picture of the house opposite and I saw his car go by. Toby's mother was driving and there was another lady sitting in the passenger seat next to her. Toby was sitting glumly in the back with a tie on. I think that he may have been heading to church. Toby's mother had always been quite religious and since Toby's father disappeared her attendance at church had increased, much to Toby's annoyance.

None of the boys targeted by the fabulous fruit flinger the previous week had made any mention of those events. Mind you, a weekend can be a long time when you're at school, and the events of the previous week can often seem a distant memory. At one point, though, during lunch, Terry Staton passed behind Leroy and quietly emptied the dregs of his water bottle onto his head.

Leroy's hair is very thick and he didn't notice the water until some seconds later when a big drop fell from his fringe onto the cheese sandwich he was eating. He leaped to his feet and started freaking out, waving his sandwich about and patting all over his head and back with his spare hand. Stinks, some distance away by then, turned around to watch him and started laughing. The rest of us started getting alarmed by the extent of Leroy's reaction.

"Take it easy, Leroy," said Toby. "It's only a bit of water, for crying out loud."

Leroy stopped suddenly and said, "What's that?"

Theo leaned over and tugged at his shirt in an effort to get him to sit down. "It's only water, Leroy, water. You know, from a water bottle. Stinks poured a bit on your head when he walked past."

"Oh, did he now?" fumed Leroy, waving a clenched fist at Stinks' departing back. "Water eh? I thought a bird had pooped on me. Right onto my head."

"Oh that's just gross, man," said Toby. "On your head – yuk!"

"Well, that wouldn't have been too bad. I could have handled that. But it went on my sandwich as well. I don't want that happening again."

We all laughed at that. Several months ago we had been sitting on the grass in the quadrangle having our lunch. A bird had flown over and dropped its scummy load and by sheer chance it landed on Leroy's honey sandwich as it traversed the space between his lunchbox and his mouth.

Leroy had been busy watching Mr Harvey holding a misbehaving pre-primary boy's head under the tap across the quadrangle at the time and hadn't noticed the noxious addition to his sandwich. He took a huge bite and within two seconds he was retching and groaning and wiping his mouth and tongue all over the lawn. Then he was up on his feet and running across the quadrangle. He tried for the water fountains first but there was a queue for those so he made for the nearby tap. Mr Harvey was still using that to discipline the recalcitrant boy, however, and waved Leroy away with his foot. It was then that Leroy remembered his water bottle and came running back to us. Of course, we were all rolling about with laughter having a great old time at his expense.

Stinks kept his distance from us in class and thankfully Wayne Galbraith and the others seemed more interested in bickering among themselves than with us. Whiner kept on taking Scabby's ruler and hitting Alphabet with it, and Galbraith seemed uninterested in anything that was going on in class. He just sat looking at his hands on the desk in front of him or stared off into space.

Mr Cranston was having one of his 'off' days as well. That was his description, not mine. On one of his 'off' days Mr Cranston would, at some point, just give the class a whole bunch of maths problems to solve, or make us write a long story or make us do an hour or more of USSR (uninterrupted, sustained, silent reading).

During those times Mr Cranston would just doodle on whatever piece of paper he had in front of him or sit gazing out of the window. Once he started doodling when we were doing a comprehension test and he was marking some of our maths homework. When I received my booklet back from him it was covered in crude drawings of motorcycles doing wheelies and what looked like zombies stepping onto land mines and being blown to bits.

After what seemed an eternity the school siren sounded and our mission to Mr Richardson's house was able to commence. The four of us lugged our schoolbags across the oval and through the trees towards the river. We had told our parents that we would be going to each other's houses after school and therefore would not require lifts home. So we had an hour or two to play with.

I'm not sure how the others felt but I was as nervous as anything. Theo and Toby seemed to be putting on a brave face, and Leroy was positively enthusiastic, but I'm sure that all of them were pretty nervous as well.

Two hundred metres downstream from the perimeter of the school was a low footbridge where we crossed the river. We then made our way back along the other side of the river towards Mr Richardson's house. There were far fewer people living on this side of the river and most of the houses were on large blocks surrounded by trees, shrubs and well-watered lawns. It was an expensive part of town, according to my father. Some of the houses had substantial fences surrounding them and some had none. All of the houses were set well back from the road.

A few minutes after crossing the river we arrived at the front of Mr Richardson's house. Many of the houses in the area were very large and undoubtedly luxurious but Mr Richardson's house seemed a relatively modest dwelling. Some of its more ostentatious neighbours reeked of wealth and rose high above their surroundings as though seeking to dominate the landscape.

Mr Richardson's house had a more restrained look and feel. His house was smallish, single-storied and built low to the ground. It had a traditional elevation and stood on a large unfenced block. It had light grey walls, dark grey window frames and the green roof that could be seen from the school oval. It was surrounded by neat gardens.

Standing in front of the house, where the long driveway met the narrow road, it was hard to determine whether the owner was out or at home. There were no cars or people around and there was no sign of activity.

"This is stupid," I said as we stood there uncertainly. "We should never have agreed to this."

"Don't be such a sook," said Leroy.

Toby's earlier bravery had dissipated. Now he appeared to share my view. He scratched his head and kicked at a rock on the ground.

"What shall we do?" asked Toby. "I don't like this. Maybe we should go home. Maybe we can tell Mr Viner that we came here but we didn't see anything unusual."

Theo shook his head. "That's not going to do and you

know it, Toby. He won't be satisfied with that. There's something going on here. Something that Mr Viner and the government doesn't like. But they can't do anything about it yet. You heard what he said. He needs us to find out what it is."

"But that's crazy," said Toby. "It doesn't make any sense. You can see what's going on at the house from here. Any cop can see."

"So what's going on?" asked Leroy.

"Nothing's going on, you bozo. That's what's going on. Nothing. It's all normal. He doesn't even have a fence. And anyway why send us? Why send a bunch of kids?"

"He explained that, Toby," said Theo. "The government can't just go marching in on people like that. They can't go up to someone's house and poke their head through the window. They need a reason. There's a process they have to follow. They need evidence and warrants and things."

"But they're always kicking down doors and busting into people's houses. Every time I watch the news they're doing it to someone."

"They can only do that when they have a reason. Like when they have a warrant or something. Until they have those they can't do anything. Their hands are tied. That's why they need us. Kids are expected to go wandering around. Kids are expected to poke their noses around and snoop. If kids get caught it doesn't matter."

I could have argued with Theo for hours over that point but I didn't bother. Now was not the time. But I agreed with Toby. He was right to be worried. This whole thing didn't feel right to me. Something was going on here that I didn't like and I didn't understand.

Leroy took a step forward. "Look gang, we've been given a deadly mission. You heard what Whiner's dad said. If we don't do it we're going to end up being sorry. It's not that hard, remember. Let's just do it and get it over with."

No one said anything in response. We all just stood there, shifting our weight from one foot to the other or fiddling with the straps of our bags. Finally Theo broke the silence. "Leroy's right," he said. "Let's get it over with. We'll just walk up to the door and knock on it. If the guy's at home we'll say we're selling cookies or something."

"We don't have any cookies," I said.

"Right," said Theo, with a sigh.

"I have half a gingerbread man left over from lunch," said Toby.

"Brilliant," said Leroy. "Why didn't I think of that? We can tell him we're selling half-eaten gingerbread men."

"Watch it, pinhead, or you'll get a thump."

"Try it, blubber-guts, and I'll bust your head."

"Take it easy," said Theo. "Okay, we'll say we need sponsors for the school walkathon. Maybe he'll agree and let us in. If he refuses I'll ask him for a drink of water. Maybe he'll let us in then. If not we'll just leave. Okay? And if he's not in we'll just take a walk around the back and maybe look in some windows. Nothing more. Agreed?"

"Agreed," said Leroy.

Theo and Leroy turned to Toby and myself and started eyeballing us belligerently. Theo pushed his glasses up a little on his nose.

"Umm . . . well . . . okay," said Toby. "But I have to say that I'm not happy."

"You don't have to be happy, you just have to do it,"

said Theo. "And you?"

"All right," I said. "But I'm with Toby on this. I'm not happy either. Let's do this quickly and get out of here."

"Okay, about time. Don't worry, it will be quick. Quick and easy. Let's go." Theo started walking up the driveway with Leroy.

Theo had changed a little since the day of his barbecue. I had never known him to be this reckless. He could do stupid things at times and sometimes he could be quite brave, but he wasn't normally reckless. I think that Mr Viner may have suckered him good and proper with his guff about hidden sequences. He had given Theo a taste and Theo wanted more. When it came to scientific stuff and the quest for further knowledge, especially secret or forbidden further knowledge, Theo was insatiable.

Toby and I followed a few paces behind them.

"If this guy turns out to be a nut I'm going to bolt," muttered Toby. I nodded and gave him a pat on the back.

"Me too, Toby. I'll be right behind you. We can trip up Leroy and then take off. But don't worry about it. It doesn't even look as though he's here. The place looks deserted."

The house and gardens were certainly very neat and tidy. There was no junk or mess lying around. No leaves on the driveway. No savage dog hell-bent on tearing the throats out of four juvenile trespassers.

Which was a great relief to me.

But the house seemed unusually quiet and still. None of the windows appeared to be open and the garage door looked as though it hadn't been opened in a long while.

When we came up to the house we stood there for a moment looking at it. Then Theo climbed the steps to the front veranda. At the door he turned around and beckoned to us. We hesitated.

"Come on, you yellow-bellied rabble. I'm not going to do this by myself!"

We slowly climbed the steps and stood behind Theo as he rang the doorbell. I could feel my heart thudding in my chest and I thought that if I strained my ears I might have heard three other hearts thumping as well.

We heard nothing from the house. No voices, no footsteps, no dogs barking or cats meowing. Theo rang the doorbell a second time.

Still nothing.

Nothing was happening. As the seconds ticked by I could feel the tension draining away from all of us and the thudding in my chest slowly subsided.

"No one home," said Leroy.

"No," agreed Theo.

"Oh, thank goodness for that," sighed Toby. "What a relief. I thought I was going to wet my pants."

Theo put his head up close to the door and tried to look through an inlaid pane of coloured glass. He shook his head. "I can't see anything." Then he moved to the window beside the door and tried peering through that.

"Nothing."

The other front windows were the same. Suddenly emboldened, we all started squinting at the windows. All of the glass seemed to be covered in some kind of tint or reflective film. If you managed to find a crack or somewhere to see through all you were faced with were closed, heavy curtains.

"This is useless," said Theo. "Let's try around the back."

"Can't we just leave?" pleaded Toby, his fear returning. "I'm going to wet my pants if we go around there."

Theo and Leroy ignored him and started to make their way around the side of the house. My feelings were aligned with Toby's but as Theo's best friend and the chronicler of his life I felt that I had no choice but to follow them. I didn't want to but I couldn't back out.

"Wait, wait," whispered Toby as he came up and fell into step beside me, grabbing at my arm nervously.

The garage was built into the left hand side of the house, if viewing it from the front, so we made our way around the other side where most of the windows were. Theo and Leroy peered into each one that they passed.

There was still nothing to see.

All of the windows were tinted and heavily curtained. At least we could tell Mr Viner that. It was better than nothing, but not much better. If nothing else, though, it would prove to him that we had been to Mr Richardson's house. We had tried, at least.

When Theo and Leroy turned the corner and came to the back of the house they stopped abruptly. Toby and I joined them and saw what had caught their attention. The first window along was partially open, but its interior was dark. I felt a sudden sinking feeling.

We all looked carefully around the back garden. Apart from a dozen or more fruit trees, what looked like a chicken coop and row upon row of vegetables there was nothing much to see. Everything looked rather ordinary, and like the front of the house it was all very neat and tidy.

Toby clutched at my arm again. "What kind of nut grows so much fruit and vegetables?" he whispered. "There must be tons of it here. Why doesn't he just go to the shops? And chickens! What's with the chickens? This guy's a raving lunatic."

I shook his hand off my arm. "Relax, Toby. It's not that abnormal. He's got a big garden. Some people like doing this kind of stuff. Maybe he eats a lot of fruit. Maybe he likes fresh eggs and vegetables. Maybe he doesn't like shopping."

We watched as Theo took his schoolbag from his shoulder and put it on the ground. Crouching down, he opened it and reached inside. He rummaged around for a moment and when his hand emerged it was holding a small torch. Then Leroy tapped Theo on the shoulder and held his hand up like a policeman. Ah, I thought, the universal signal for 'stop'. All of a sudden they had both gone very quiet.

Toby and I froze. There was silence. It was deathly still. Apart from a dog barking some distance away and a truck changing gears noisily somewhere to our north I couldn't hear a thing. Then Toby's stomach rumbled, Theo sneezed and a jet flew overhead. Okay, then, there might have been a bit of noise. But apart from all that there was silence.

Leroy turned to us and put the index finger of his right hand to his lips. Ah, I thought, it's another universal signal. This signal was a bit more ambiguous, as it could have two meanings. The first and most common interpretation usually meant 'be quiet'. Generally it was employed with a frown and the eyes directed forwards. The second interpretation meant something like 'hmm, now where did I leave it?' This was usually delivered with a blank expression and the eyes directed towards the sky.

In our current situation I had to assume that Leroy's signal was of the first variety, and this was confirmed by the frown on his face and the direction of his eyes. Leroy was definitely up to something. There was an intensity about him that was usually only apparent when he was dying to go to the toilet or when someone was about to get their head busted.

We all stood quietly and still as Leroy rummaged around in his school bag. When his hand emerged it was clutching a vicious looking knife with a blade about a foot long. Theo instantly went pale and looked as though he was about to faint. My stomach jumped and lurched and Toby yelped in terror beside me.

"I'm going to wet my pants," he squeaked, running around in a circle looking for somewhere to hide.

What in heaven's name was Leroy doing with that awful thing in his bag? I couldn't believe my eyes. The thing was obscene. It was an abomination. It was nearly as big as he was. What the heck was he thinking? What was it with these two? Torches and knives?

Knives?

What else did they have in those bags? Or concealed on their persons? It didn't bear thinking about.

If I put *my* hand in *my* schoolbag and rummaged around all that I would come out with would be half a sandwich or an apple core. If Toby did the same I'd expect something similar. It certainly wouldn't be a torch or a knife. Even Theo, pumped up as he was, was appalled at the sight of Leroy's hideous weapon.

"Gotterdammerung!"

"Eh?" queried Leroy.

"What are you doing with that thing, Leroy? Are you completely nuts? Where did you get that thing? A knife that big just has to be illegal. And having it in your bag is illegal as well. I can't believe you brought that to school. Put that away right now and don't take it out again!"

I'd never heard Theo swear before and I didn't know what it meant but I was relieved to see that he hadn't fully taken leave of his senses. If Theo suddenly went bananas we'd be in real trouble.

Leroy growled in annoyance and waved the knife around menacingly. Then he stopped, looked at the knife wistfully, gave a big sigh and then put it back in his bag.

"All right, all right," he hissed. "But if we get attacked it's coming out again."

"Yes, yes," said Theo.

"I mean it," said Leroy.

"All right, Leroy, now shut up," replied Theo.

Thank heavens for that, I thought, as Leroy zipped up his bag. I never wanted to see that thing again. Sanity, or at least partial sanity, had been restored to the operation. I started to breathe again and Toby stopped running around in circles.

With his knife back in his bag Leroy crept up to the window with Theo. Toby and I stayed well back taking a strategically sound rearguard position. We were both extremely jumpy and ready to bolt in an instant.

Theo and Leroy peered in the window. After a moment Theo lifted his hand and shone his torch in there.

I could tell just by looking at the back of their heads that they could see nothing of interest. If you're observant, and perceptive, you can tell a lot from the back of someone's head. Far more than you might think. You should try it some time.

Leaving the open window, Theo and Leroy kept walking, trying each of the back windows in turn. They came to the back door and Leroy, in a fit of what can only be described as absolute lunacy, turned the handle and gave it a gentle push.

To our surprise, and not to mention horror, the door opened a crack. We were stunned.

"*Garammasala* – *it's not locked!*" blurted Theo, stating the obvious and clutching at Leroy's arm.

"Theo, will you please stop swearing," I muttered. "You're making me very nervous."

"What do we do?" asked Leroy, pointing at the door.

Theo let go of Leroy and stared at the partially opened door. He thought for a moment. "Let's go in," he said, grimly.

"*WHAT?*" wailed Toby. "Are you completely nuts? Are you out of your tiny flipping mind? This is just crazy. It's mind-blowingly, teeth-grindingly, butt-clenchingly crazy. That's it, I'm really going to wet my pants now. You asked for it. It's coming, I can feel it."

"Shut up, Toby," snapped Leroy. "This is what we came for. This is what Viner wants. This is where our deadly mission really begins."

"Leroy, will you *please* stop saying that?" pleaded Toby.

"Saying what?" asked Leroy.

"*Deadly,*" said Toby.

"All right, all right, take it easy."

"Right guys," said Theo. "Relax, Toby. Just chill out, will you? Let's get in and out quickly. Thirty seconds to look around and then we're done."

"I'm not going in there," said Toby, shaking his head and backing away from the porch. "No way. Never. Not in a million years."

"Okay," said Theo. "Then you stay out here and keep watch. Come on guys." He pushed open the back door and stepped carefully inside. Leroy and I followed him.

"Hey wait! Hang on, wait for me," squawked Toby and he hurried in after us.

It was very gloomy inside the house. None of the lights were on and most of the windows that we could see had their curtains closed. Theo thought about switching on a light and reached out for what looked like a nearby switch but then thought better of it.

We were standing in the laundry, and beyond the laundry door was a hallway leading into the main part of the house. Aside from a trough and an old washer and dryer the laundry contained a shower and a doorway which opened into a powder room.

"Remember, guys," whispered Theo. "Whatever you do make sure you don't touch anything. This is supremely important. Don't touch a single flipping thing. We don't want things moved and we don't want to leave any fingerprints." Then he pointed towards the rest of the house and crept, as quietly as a cat, through the door into the hallway.

Leroy took his hand off the glass shower screen and followed Theo. Toby put down the screwdriver he had found lying by the trough and tip-toed after Leroy. I dropped the aviation magazine I had just picked up back onto the pile near the back door and followed up the rear.

The house was extremely quiet. It was quiet and gloomy. Gloomy and quiet.

From the laundry we made our way through the kitchen and family room towards the front of the house. It was dark in the centre of the house so Theo used his torch to light the way. As per Mr Viner's instructions we were looking for anything out of the ordinary, but so far I hadn't seen anything that struck me as unusual. The house was unusually dark, perhaps, but that was only because all of the curtains were closed. If they were opened, or the lights were put on, the house would probably appear quite normal. Simply and sparsely furnished, perhaps, but still quite normal.

It was only as we approached the front rooms of the house that things began to feel a little strange. I think that the others felt it too because Theo, who was still in the lead, turned off his torch and slowed his movements right down.

We stopped for a few seconds to gain our bearings and let our eyes adjust to the dark. With nobody moving the house was deathly still and quiet. Our nerves were taut and our ears strained for even the slightest noise. There was nothing to be heard.

At that moment I began to feel a kind of presence in the house. It was like that strange feeling you sometimes get when someone is watching you or when a coconut is about to fall out of a tree and land on your head. At the same time I noticed a faint smell in the air, an unusual medicinal or chemical smell that seemed to be slowly getting stronger.

"Toby," I whispered as loudly as I dared. "Was that you?"

Toby's response was also a whisper, but even so there was no mistaking the pain and outrage in his voice. "No, that was not me!" he hissed. "How insulting! Have you no manners? You can't just go around accusing people like that. It's very rude. It most certainly was *not* me. It must have been Leroy."

"Where are you, fat boy? I'm gonna bust your head good and proper."

"I'm over there, pinhead. Up front where the action is. What's the matter, can't see without your night-vision glasses?"

"Right, that does it!"

I heard a brief scuffle and then the distinct sounds of a slap and a thump. Then there was a muffled cry of pain.

"*Ow!* Leroy, that was me, you idiot," Theo complained. "Toby's back there. Cut it out!"

"Sorry, Theo," whispered Leroy. I heard another thump.

"*OW!* That was me again! Stop it, Leroy!"

"Sorry, Theo. Where are you Toby, you slug?"

"I'm over there, Leroy."

"Where?"

"There, dimwit."

"*Where?*"

"*There!*"

"That's a hat stand, you imbecile. Where are you, stinky-boy?"

"Will you all shut up," ordered Theo in a thick and frenzied whisper. "Just stop mucking about. This is serious stuff and it's not the time to be messing about. Listen, that smell is coming from in here."

Theo was standing next to a closed door not far from

the front door of the house. Some light filtered in through the glass panels in the door, but it wasn't much.

"Don't open that door," whispered Toby. "Whatever you do don't open it. I'm not going through that door. No way. Not in a million years."

"We have to," replied Theo. "Whatever Viner wants is behind this door, it has to be. There's nothing else here. We need to know what it is. We need to know what's behind this door."

"No, we don't."

"Yes, we do."

"No, we don't!"

"Yes, we do!"

"Theo's right," whispered Leroy. "Shut up, Toby, or you'll get a double thump when I can finally see you. Open it, Theo, open the flipping door. Go on, do it."

Theo counted softly to three and then opened the door. We filed in slowly, our senses on red alert and our nerves stretched as taut as a length of piano wire attaching an elephant to a helicopter.

Like the rest of the house the room was dark inside. But the feel of this room was oppressive and the chemical smell was much stronger. It was almost overpowering. I could feel myself starting to feel faint.

"I've smelt this before," whispered Leroy. "I know I have. I can't remember where and I can't remember when. But I have smelt it. I know it."

"What is it?" breathed Theo.

"I just can't remember."

"Will you both shut up," hissed Toby.

"Wait," said Leroy. "I know what it is – I know what it

is. It's the smell . . . it's the smell . . . of . . . *death!*"

"*What?*" squawked Toby, in a tiny voice that sounded as though he was being sat on by a giant gorilla and strangled.

Theo switched the torch on, and then with an almighty crash the door suddenly slammed behind us.

"Got you," said a silky voice, and we all screamed.

Chapter 10

Mr Richardson

After the screams died down the light was switched on and we could see what was happening. My first impression was that the room looked quite normal with the light on; there was nothing sinister about it at all.

Theo and Leroy, though, were hugging each other in a blind panic, their faces contorted with terror. If I wasn't so terrified myself I probably would have thought the sight comical. I found myself clutching Toby, who had his arms wound so tightly around my midriff that I could barely breathe. I expect that we looked comical as well.

We were huddled together in the middle of a large study. There were books along all of the walls and leaning up against the door was a slightly built, balding man in spectacles and a yellow cardigan. He had an amused smile on his face but I knew that meant nothing. Everyone with a television knew that the standard expression of most of the world's deranged killers and psychopaths was an amused smile. It was especially true when they were just about to dispatch someone horribly, using ropes and knives and pain and all that.

Most of the world's deranged killers and psychopaths also probably wore yellow cardigans as well. I mean, why else would you wear one?

"Scared you, did I?" observed the balding, yellow-cardiganed psychopath and/or deranged killer. "Well, you deserve it. You deserve it good and proper. What are you playing at? What on earth are you doing creeping around my house? And making such a terrible racket as well? I don't know if you were trying to be quiet, but they could probably hear you across the river."

So this was Mr Richardson. He sounded a bit annoyed, but not particularly angry. And he still had that smile on his face.

"Umm, may I use the toilet, please?" squeaked Toby. "Otherwise I'm going to wet my pants."

"You look as though you need to," said Mr Richardson, moving away from the door and opening it.

"I do, really I do."

"Go on then, use the one in the laundry. The one near the back door. But make sure you come back here. Don't take off. Remember that I've got your friends in here as hostages. Run away and they're for it."

"Yes, sir," said Toby, letting go of me and hurrying out of the room. Great, I thought. He'll probably bolt and then we're for it. But maybe he would come back. I hoped that he would.

While he was gone Theo and Leroy slowly untangled themselves and Mr Richardson bent down to retrieve Theo's torch from the floor. He switched it off and handed it to Theo. He was still favouring us with an amused smile. Either he was in jovial spirits, which was a good sign, or he was in full-blown psycho mode and was about to unleash all of his pain and madness upon us. Naturally I hoped for the former.

While Toby was away using the amenities I took the opportunity to have a quick look around the room. Aside from the bookshelves there were two desks, a chair on wheels and a computer. On one of the walls was a chart showing the layout of the solar system and on another was a big poster of the periodic table of the elements.

We have a similar poster in our classroom at school which we use for our 'explorations in chemistry' subject. Mr Cranston often stood in front of it with a big ruler, pointing out the elements he liked best (Arsenic, Berkelium and Boron) and giggling to himself whenever he wrote out the symbols for Holmium and Polonium.

On top of some of the bookshelves, and suspended on thin wires from the ceiling, were a number of model aeroplanes. All right, I thought, Mr Viner will be pleased. We're starting to get a bit of a picture of Mr Richardson now. A hint of his character and personality.

One of the desks was covered with an assortment of glues and paints on a sheet of newspaper, and the plastic parts of an unfinished Bristol Beaufighter. Don't ask me how I knew that, but I did. Nearly all boys my age, after all, and even a few girls, are knowledgeable about those kinds of things.

So much for the smell of death, Leroy.

You knucklehead. It was nothing but the smell of modelling paint and glue. Perhaps a hint of popcorn, as well, although I couldn't be certain about that.

The smell of death . . . ha!

It was death to a plastic Luftwaffe, perhaps. Or death to a plastic German army and navy. But nothing more than that.

Theo and Leroy were also looking around the room and were looking similarly abashed. There was nothing sinister in this study at all.

Nothing.

Unless you'd consider a Stuka poised and about to release its lethal payload over a copy of *Pride and Prejudice* sinister. Maybe someone obsessive and suspicious like Whiner's dad might, but I didn't.

Mr Richardson stood watching us while we waited for Toby to return. When Toby came back, looking relieved that we were all still breathing, Mr Richardson took us through to the living room. He told us to take a seat on the couch and opened the curtains. Late afternoon light flooded into the room. I started to feel a whole lot better.

Mr Richardson took a seat opposite us. He surveyed us carefully and started squeezing gently at his neck. Maybe he had a sore throat or something.

"Right then, you still haven't answered my question. What are you doing, sneaking around in my house? It is against the law, you know. People get sent to jail for doing things like that. What were you thinking? What were you doing?"

None of us said anything.

"Look, there's no need to worry," Mr Richardson continued, with a resigned sigh. "You're not going to get into trouble. I can see that you meant no harm. I can see that you're all harmless."

Leroy, who was sitting next to me, start to bristle a bit at this. I knew exactly what he was thinking. He was thinking of the knife in his bag and his mind was churning over the concept *"me . . . harmless?"*

I gave Leroy a quick nudge with my elbow to keep him quiet. Mr Richardson seemed quite benign for now; no good would come from aggravating him.

"Umm," said Theo, "then you're not going to tell our parents?"

"I should, I guess, but I won't," replied Mr Richardson.

"You're not going to call the police?"

"No."

"You're not going to kill us?"

"Good grief, that's only third on your list of worries? Dear me. Well, perhaps I should kill you, then call the police, and then tell your parents."

Toby, sitting on my other side, went "Huh?" and gave a little whimper.

Mr Richardson smiled and shook his head. "No, I'm not going to kill you, or call the police, or your parents, or your school, or anything. I'd just like to know why you're here. Why you came into my garden and why you came into my house. Tell me that and you're free to go. I mean it. You'll be free to go."

"All right," said Theo, looking relieved. "We'll tell you. I don't see why we can't. Mr Viner said we could speak to you, but he didn't say anything about not saying anything."

Mr Richardson frowned at this. "I'm not sure I fully got that," he said, "but I did hear you say Mr Viner. Who is this Mr Viner?"

Before any of us could answer Mr Richardson stood up abruptly. "Gosh, where are my manners?" he asked himself. "Would any of you like a drink? Maybe a biscuit or two? I don't have much, but I do know that young kids are usually famished straight after school. Don't worry, I promise you won't be drugged or poisoned or anything horrible like that. Scout's honour."

"Okay," said Theo. "I'd love a drink, thank you."

After Mr Richardson gave us each a glass of orange juice and put a plate of biscuits onto the coffee table before us we told him our names and why we had come to his house. Theo did most of the explaining, with the rest of us interrupting when we thought he had left something important out.

After we'd finished Mr Richardson leaned back in his chair, closed his eyes and clasped his palms together. He looked as though he was praying, or having a nap, but I'm pretty sure he was just thinking. After a minute he nodded and scratched his head.

"I thought there must have been more to it," he said, almost to himself. "I know that kids your age don't normally do this kind of stuff."

Mr Richardson opened his eyes and looked at us. "I knew you were up to something from the start," he said. "Occasionally I get school kids around here causing a bit of mischief or pinching a piece of fruit. I don't mind that. Kids are kids. If they want a few of my apples or mandarins they're welcome to them. But I don't often get four kids, still in school uniform, lined up like statues across the bottom of my driveway. I was sitting in my study and I saw you down there and I wondered what on earth you were doing. Then I watched you come up to the house. When you knocked I was about to answer the door but then I thought I'd wait and see what you did next. I'm glad that I did."

"We were only doing what Mr Viner told us to," said Leroy. "We weren't going to do anything or take anything. We didn't mean any harm."

"I know you didn't, Larry. I know that you were just following instructions. This Mr Viner's instructions."

"I'm Leroy."

"So sorry, I meant to say Leroy. You were just following Mr Viner's instructions, Leroy."

"That's right," said Toby eagerly, while helping himself to another biscuit. "We were just following instructions."

"You know, kids," said Mr Richardson, "I'm glad you're here. I was expecting something to happen, but I didn't know what it would be. Now I have a better idea of what it might be."

"What do you mean?" asked Theo.

"Well, Theo, I've been getting an odd feeling lately, a feeling of unease. A few weeks ago I rode my bike to the supermarket and as I was locking it up at the racks I saw a man in a grey suit get out of a nearby car. I only noticed him because the car was similar to one I had seen parked on the street outside my house earlier that day. Anyway, I went into the supermarket to get a few things and as I was strolling down the aisle this man came up to me with a clipboard in his hand. He introduced himself and said that the supermarket was doing some research on its product lines and did I have a moment to spare. He just wanted to ask me a few questions about my lifestyle and the type of shopping experience I was after."

"What did you say to him?" asked Theo.

"I told him that I was in a hurry and walked away. I made my purchases quickly and then I left."

"So what did he want?" asked Toby.

"I don't know, specifically," said Mr Richardson. "But obviously he wanted to know something about me. Now I'm a rather private person, as you've probably guessed. I keep to myself and I expect others to keep their distance. And I knew that this man didn't work for the supermarket. I'm not an idiot. I mean I'd seen him get out of his car and follow me in there. I suspect he might have been one of your Mr Viner's colleagues."

"But why are they interested in you?" asked Theo. "What have you done? And why should they send us?"

"I think I might know the answers to all of those questions, Theo. Let me tell you a little bit about myself. When I was younger I used to work in computers. I worked mainly with databases and I was pretty good at what I did. The company I worked for did a lot of work with the government and the military. I was a good employee and I was making quite a bit of money. My area of specialty was the extraction of meaning from huge volumes of data. You know, identifying trends, honing in on certain patterns, that sort of thing. I won't bore you with the details."

"My mother works on stuff like that," said Theo. "She does work for the government, too, and she knows Mr Viner."

Mr Richardson raised an eyebrow and took a bite of his biscuit. "What's your surname, Theo?" he asked. Theo told him.

"Thorne, eh? Well, that makes sense. Things are starting to fall into place now. Anyway, the work we were doing was becoming more and more interesting to more and more people but I wasn't too happy with the direction it was going. Up until then I had been identifying things like how many phone calls were being made, or how many people bought a certain type of car or book. Then things started to change and I was being asked to identify who was making those phone calls and who was buying those cars or those books. That was not something that I wanted to do."

"Why not?" asked Leroy. "Who cares? What's the difference?"

"The difference, Larry, is that at the start I was only being asked to find out stuff about things. You know, inanimate objects. Which was fine. But then they wanted me to find out stuff about people. Stuff that was none of my business and none of the company's business, either. Or the government's business. I couldn't do it. So I gave it all up. I have simple needs and a reasonable amount of money stashed away. I quit my job and moved over here. To live a quiet, peaceful life. To read books and look after my garden."

"And make your model aeroplanes," said Leroy.

"Yes, and to make my model aeroplanes," agreed Mr Richardson.

"So why is Mr Viner interested in you?" asked Theo.

Mr Richardson was quiet for a moment. He tapped his finger against his lip a few times. I took a sip of my orange juice and a bite of my biscuit. It was chocolate and it had a thin layer of jam and cream inside it. Very tasty.

"To be honest, I don't really think that Mr Viner is all

that interested in me. Not in me directly, anyway. But he is interested in people like me. You see, the world is changing, and changing very quickly too. You're probably too young to notice it. Now I don't much like the way the world is going and there are others like me as well."

"My dad hates the way the world is going," said Leroy.

"Hmm. A lot of people, like Mr Viner, will tell you that things are getting better and better, that people have more freedom now than they've ever had before. But I think the opposite is true. We're not getting freer at all. We're getting less free. We're being hemmed into cages of data and people like Mr Viner are holding all of the keys. You young folk know all about computers and the internet but there's another invisible net around us, a more sinister one. This net is gathering all sorts of information about everyone and it's getting tighter with each passing day. But not everyone wants their information collected and stored in this way. I certainly don't."

"An invisible net," murmured Leroy.

"Yes," said Mr Richardson.

"Cool," said Leroy.

"Well, I don't think it is very cool, actually."

"Oh, okay," said Leroy. "So it's all the computers . . ."

"Yes."

"Like all those little RFID tags and readers," I said, remembering what Theo had told me after the exploding mobile phone episode.

"That's exactly so," said Mr Richardson. "They're just one example. We're surrounded by all sorts of instruments that do nothing but gather information about us, each and every one of us. Sure, all this stuff might make it easier for us to buy . . . say . . . a pair of shoes, but is that really what we need? Do they need to know everything about us to help us buy a new pair of sneakers?"

"Probably not," ventured Theo tentatively.

"Exactly. And it's making us dumber at the same time. You don't even need to remember your shoe size anymore. You can walk into any shoe store and the tag reader will know the size of the shoe you're wearing and the type of shoe it is. The tag reader will link to the database which records where you bought the shoe from, who you are and the kinds of clothes and things that you like. Based on all this information the tag reader can spit out a bit of paper containing everything about you and the type of shoes that would probably appeal to you. You don't have to think or do anything. The shop assistant doesn't have to think or do anything. All they have to do is walk up to you and say 'here are the type of shoes that you're after,' whether you're after them or not. I mean, you might have entered the shop to buy a can of shoe polish. Is this the kind of world you want? Is this giving you greater freedom?"

"Probably not," ventured Theo again, although this time with a little more conviction.

Mr Richardson stood up, walked over to the window and spent some time looking out at the view across the river. In the distance a dog started barking. Maybe it was the same one that had been barking earlier. I saw a large grey bird fly by. No nets around that creature, I thought.

We all sat still and considered what Mr Richardson had been saying to us. Leroy yawned and scratched his belly and Theo took the final biscuit from the plate in front of him. After a further minute or so Mr Richardson returned to his chair and sat down.

"Do you know why this Mr Viner person wanted you to come here?" he asked.

"No," I replied.

"He wanted you to come here because he no longer knows anything about me and that's enough to make a man like him suspicious. I don't appear in any of his databases anymore. I don't have a telephone or a mobile phone. My computer is no longer connected to the internet."

"What?" cried Leroy in disbelief.

Mr Richardson smiled. "That's right. I don't have the internet here. I don't have a car either and I got rid of all my credit cards months ago. I use cash wherever I can and I destroy the RFID tags of everything I purchase."

"Wow," said Theo, quietly.

"Yes, it is pretty extreme, isn't it? But believe me, it's the only way to go if you want to keep a low profile."

"But why would you go to all that bother? Are you trying to hide?" asked Theo.

"No," replied Mr Richardson.

"Are you trying to disappear?" This was from Toby, all eager, his glass of orange juice suspended in mid-transit between the coffee table and his mouth.

"No, I'm not trying to disappear."

"So what does Mr Viner want?"

"Mr Viner doesn't care for people like me. In fact he hates people like me. Mr Viner wants to be able to tap someone's name into his computer and have everything about them appear before his eyes. Their family, their friends, their financial details, where they go and what they do. He wants to know the movies they like and the books they read. He wants to see their medical records, read transcripts of every phone conversation they have ever had, see a history of every web site they have ever visited and get a list of every purchase they have ever made. There is never enough information for the likes of Mr Viner. So when he punches a name into his computer and not much comes up he gets suspicious. There's no thought that maybe this person just lives a very low-key life or just wants a bit of peace and quiet. There's no thought that this person might just like their privacy. Oh no, it's never that. For people like him it's always: what is this person trying to hide?"

Mr Richardson fell silent and for a moment or two he looked very sad and weary. He started squeezing gently at his neck again. He buttoned up his cardigan, looked down at what he'd done and then unbuttoned it.

For a full minute nobody spoke. Then Theo, who was starting to feel a bit uncomfortable, thought he had better say something.

"Mr Richardson, before school tomorrow Mr Viner is going to find us and ask us what happened here. What should we say to him?"

"You're a good kid, Theo. I can see that you're all really good kids. I think that Mr Viner is going to want to hear something that he can use against me. He'll want to hear that my house is full of guns or drugs, or that I tried to touch you inappropriately. Just tell him the truth, Theo. Tell him that I'm ashamed of my contribution to the kind of work that he does. Tell him that I like reading my books, riding my bicycle, and tending to my fruit and vegetables. Tell him that all I crave is some peace and quiet. Can you do that, Theo?"

"Of course we can do that, Mr Richardson. We can tell him that. No problem. You can count on us."

"I knew that I could. It doesn't have to be word for word; just the gist of it is fine. And I think you've got the gist of it. I knew you were good kids."

Mr Richardson stood up and started picking up our glasses. Toby slid the biscuit tray across the table to him.

"Off you go now," said Mr Richardson. "Your parents are probably wondering where you are."

"We're very sorry we disturbed you, Mr Richardson. We're really very sorry."

"Yes, I can see that you are. Thank you, Theo."

We were all very quiet on the walk back down Mr Richardson's driveway towards the river. I was giving a great deal of thought to all of the things he had told us and I suspect the others were as well. Toby was the first to break the silence.

"What a crackpot!" he said. "That guy's a raving lunatic."

Leroy nodded in agreement. "Yes he was, wasn't he? A first class nutter. No mobile phone, no internet, no car. What a loser!"

"And all those fruit trees and vegetables," said Toby.

"Crazy."

"Slow down," said Theo. "He wasn't so bad. He seemed like a bit of a nerd, maybe, but what he was saying made sense, didn't it?"

"I thought it did," I said.

"It did make sense," said Theo. "And don't forget, he could have turned us in to the cops if he'd wanted to. Just because Mr Viner said we could go in there doesn't mean it was legal."

"Theo's right," I said. "Mr Richardson could have turned us in. He might be a nerd but at least he's not as slimy as Viner."

"I suppose not," conceded Toby.

"He's still a nutter, I reckon," said Leroy, "but Whiner's dad is worse. He's the absolute pits."

"Well, I expect we'll be seeing Mr Viner tomorrow," said Theo. "We'll see what he has to say then."

Chapter 11

Mr Viner

True to his word, Mr Viner was waiting for us when we arrived at school the next morning. He had waved his son off and was sitting in his car listening to the radio when Toby and I walked up to the gate. Off down the street we could see Theo and Leroy approaching so we waited until they joined us. Then we walked over to the car.

Mr Viner's car was a big, dark blue BMW with dark tinted windows. There was a dent in the front wing shaped like a man's head. As we drew near Mr Viner turned the radio off and climbed out of the car.

"Good morning everyone," he said. "Are you all well?"

"We are," said Theo.

"Good," he said. "All ready for school?"

"Yes," said Theo. The rest of us variously nodded or grunted.

"Good, good. That's excellent to hear. Good to see our young folk all fired up and raring to go. But enough of the boring pleasantries. So what's new? Did you have a good afternoon yesterday? How did your visit to Mr Richardson go? I know you all went there and I know you managed to get inside. What did you see? Was Richardson there? Did you speak with him? Come on then, out with it."

Mr Viner's head kept bobbing as he spoke and I saw a little bit of spittle spray through the air towards us. He really was an unpleasant piece of work.

"Mr Richardson was there," said Theo. "And yes, we spoke with him for a while."

"Wonderful!" said Mr Viner. "Wonderful. He's a strange fellow, don't you think? A very strange fellow. An odd kind of chap, in my view."

Mr Viner paused and looked up towards the school. Then he glanced at his watch. Cars were still rolling slowly through the car park and dropping off children.

"Richardson's really a bit of a nerd, I think. I actually met him once, a few years ago. He probably doesn't remember me. Well, what happened? Did he let you in or did you break in?"

"Um, we let ourselves in," said Theo, choosing his words carefully. "The back door was unlocked."

"But he knew we were coming," said Toby.

Mr Viner nodded thoughtfully. "So he knew you were coming, eh? Interesting. Okay, so then what happened? What did he do?"

"He didn't do anything," said Theo.

For an instant Mr Viner looked disappointed but then he nodded again and gave us an encouraging smile. "Go on," he said.

Theo corrected himself. "Well, he did do something. He gave us a drink and some biscuits."

"He gave you a drink and some biscuits."

"Yes."

"All right. What kind of drink?"

"Orange juice."

"What kind of biscuits?"

"Chocolate cream," said Leroy.

"Typical."

I wasn't sure what Mr Viner meant by that. What did it matter what kind of biscuits Mr Richardson had in his house? I couldn't fathom it. But Mr Viner obviously found something offensive in his biscuit selection, judging by the sour expression on his face.

"Okay, what else?"

"We sat in his living room and he talked to us."

"He talked to you?"

"Yes."

"You sat in his living room and he talked to you."

"Yes."

"And you had orange juice and some chocolate cream biscuits."

"Yes."

Mr Viner sighed and looked at his watch again. Then he waved to one of the parents walking by with two children. He turned his attention back to us.

"To be completely honest, I'm not too interested in whatever it was that Mr Richardson had to say to you. I think I can guess most of it. The ravings of a lunatic, undoubtedly. What I'm interested in is his house. What sort of things did he have inside his house? Did you notice anything unusual?"

"Well," said Theo, "he had furniture and a television . . ."

"Yes, yes," said Mr Viner.

"A washer and a dryer," said Toby.

"Come on, come on . . ."

"He had one of those round things that people use to flatten things," said Leroy.

"Flatten things? What do you mean, flatten things?"

"You know, flatten things."

"What – a sledgehammer? A shovel? A wrecking ball? Come on boy . . . a stick of dynamite?"

"You know, like when you're making something."

"Making something? Or destroying something?"

"No, making something. Like cooking."

"You mean a rolling pin?"

"That's it!"

"Oh, for heaven's sake."

Mr Viner was starting to look a bit impatient. He took off his glasses and rubbed his temples with his fingers and thumb. My father often did that when he had a rotten headache.

"Anything unusual, I said. Did you see anything unusual in the house, anything out of the ordinary?"

"He had loads of books in his study," said Leroy. "And a big chemistry poster and a poster showing all the planets. And a computer that wasn't connected to the internet."

"A chemistry poster, you say?"

"The periodic table," said Theo.

"The periodic table," repeated Mr Viner. He seemed to turn this over in his mind and he scratched his head thoughtfully.

"Of the elements," explained Theo.

"Yes, I know what it is," snapped Mr Viner. "I went to

school as well, you know. So he had lots of books in his study, did he?"

"Yes."

"Okay, so what kind of books did he have in this study of his?" asked Mr Viner.

"I dunno," said Leroy. "Reading books, what else?"

"Computer books," said Theo. "He had loads of computer books."

"And histories," I said. "Lots of histories and novels."

At this Mr Viner turned his attention to me. It was attention I could have done without, and I wished I'd kept my mouth shut.

"What kind of histories?" he asked, with a sneer. "Anything political? Or military?"

"I don't think so," I said, trying to recall some of the titles. "I can't remember."

"It doesn't matter, I suppose," said Mr Viner. "All history's political. And most of it is military as well. So was there anything else any of you can think of?" He pulled his phone out of his pocket and pressed several buttons.

"He had lots of model aeroplanes," said Theo. "Model aeroplanes are his hobby. He likes making them. He told us that all he wants is to be left alone so that he can make his models and grow his fruit and vegetables."

Mr Viner jerked his head up at this and put his phone back into his pocket. "Fruit and vegetables," he muttered, "I knew he was a nutter." He shook his head as if to clear it of cobwebs. Then his focus returned and so did his bark.

"Right then, what kinds of aeroplane models has he got?" he snapped. "How big are they?"

"Well, they're all pretty small," replied Theo. "And

they're World War Two, mainly."

"More information, please," said Mr Viner.

"Well, there was a Spitfire and a Beaufighter . . ."

"A Stuka and a Lancaster . . ."

"A Mustang . . ."

"A Stuka, you say? Very . . . interesting," he murmured, half to himself.

Now Mr Viner was looking up at the sky. It was as though he was half expecting a Stuka to come roaring out of nowhere across the heavens to unload a bomb onto the school canteen.

"You can never trust a fellow who keeps a Stuka in his house. Regardless of the size of it. That's the first thing they teach you. Were there any more German planes? What other German planes did the psycho have?"

"He's not a psycho," I said, with what I hoped was a touch of defiance in my voice. "But he did have a Messerschmitt 109," I added.

"And a Heinkel," said Toby.

"And a Dornier 23, and a Focke-Wulf Moskito," said Theo, as the school siren went off.

"Good . . . good."

"Mr Viner, we have to go now," said Leroy. "Our classes are starting."

Mr Viner had his phone back out of his pocket and was dialling a number. He nodded and said, "Yes, yes, I do know how schools generally operate."

"Can we go, then?"

"Okay, if there was nothing else out of the ordinary then I suppose you're done. You've done enough. Your mission is over. Congratulations, it was a resounding success. Keep your mouths shut and don't talk about this to anyone. One day I'll get you a ride on one of our helicopters. As long as you keep quiet and stop picking on Paul."

"We will, Mr Viner," said Leroy, shouldering his bag. He turned and started to walk to the gate. Theo and Toby walked with him.

I took a couple of paces after them then paused. Mr Viner had turned to his car with the phone pressed to his ear. He had his back to me. I was curious about who he was calling and waited.

"Reynolds," said Mr Viner, "I think that we've got enough. Political tracts, military studies, probably some Nazi regalia."

There was a pause. Mr Viner's back was still towards me. The person on the other end of the line, Reynolds, was saying something. Then it was Mr Viner's turn again.

"Books," he snapped. "Loads of histories. We can do anything we want with them. And model aeroplanes . . . I know, I know, but they're covered in swastikas. You know the drill. We don't have to say where they were. Apparently he was interested in chemistry as well. You know what that means. We can call him a white supremacist, a neo-Nazi, a danger to us all. With a bit of luck we could get a self-detonation happening."

There was another pause, longer this time. Mr Viner shifted his phone to his other ear and rested his spare hand on the roof of his car. His back was still facing me, but I could tell by the back of his head that he was getting angry. He said something low into the phone and then listened some more. Then he suddenly thumped the car roof with his fist.

"Reynolds," he said. "Give it over. I'm telling you we've got enough. Don't be such a pansy. I've wanted this one since he turned in his library card and I'm going to get him. So come and get me, right now, because we're going in."

As Mr Viner terminated the phone call and opened his car door I made my way through the gate and up the path to the classrooms. After a few seconds I turned my head to see if he'd gone. His car was still there and I could see him standing where he was, watching me. I jogged to catch up with the others.

A few minutes later we were taking to our seats in the classroom and preparing for the day ahead. Mr Cranston was at the front of the class throwing peanuts into the air and trying to catch them with his mouth. He was pretty hopeless at this and the nuts were going everywhere. The school did have a very strict 'no peanuts anywhere' policy to guard against the possibility of allergic reactions but obviously Mr Cranston didn't think that policy applied to him.

"Maths, everyone," he said. "You know the drill." We always had maths first thing on Tuesdays.

By some miracle a wayward peanut managed to find its unfortunate way into Mr Cranston's mouth. Then another. At this Mr Cranston started getting cocky. He did a little dance and tossed another peanut into the air, higher this time. It came down, bounced off his chin and headed for the front row of desks. I followed the nut's trajectory and watched as it landed in the cleft of Philip Knox's folded arms. As far as I knew he had no peanut allergy but he shrieked as though the very touch of a nut would kill him instantly. He leaped to his feet and flicked the peanut away from his desk with his ruler. Mr Cranston laughed, then pulled an imaginary pistol out of an imaginary holster at his hip and pretended to shoot Philip in the head.

It was as we were pulling our maths books and paper out of our desks that we heard the faint sound of helicopters in the distance. The sound grew louder so rapidly that Mr Cranston's coordination was thrown out of whack and the next peanut went up his nose rather than in his mouth. He reacted like he'd been shot at close range with an elephant gun. He bellowed hugely and dropped to the ground like a stone. We all took advantage of this to stand and cross over to the large windows overlooking the oval. Ignoring Mr Cranston snuffling and thrashing about on the floor we watched as a black helicopter circled the school and then landed on the damp grass. Three other helicopters remained hovering in the air some distance away.

Across the oval I could see Mr Viner standing in the car park. He took off his jacket and threw it through the open window of his car. Then he ran across the grass to the waiting helicopter and climbed aboard.

"Hey, I think that's my dad," I heard Whiner say to Galbraith.

"Rubbish," said Galbraith.

"It is."

"It is not."

"No, it is. That's our car. That blue one over there."

"What's he doing getting in a helicopter, then? I thought you said he worked in pest control," said Galbraith.

"He does . . ." said Whiner.

I couldn't hear any more of their exchange. The helicopter took off with a terrific racket and flew low across the oval in the direction of the river. The other helicopters followed. The clamour of the helicopters was gradually replaced by the sound of Mr Cranston groaning and noisily expelling a peanut from his nostril. He was covered in sweat and looked a bit green.

"Maths, then," he said weakly. "Please open your books and turn to page one hundred and sixty seven."

Chapter 12

Home Truths

It was all over the news on the following evening. With the flurry of activity around the school and the helicopters and everything we thought that there might have been some mention of an incident in the media. So after school Theo and I sat in front of the television looking out for it. My parents had gone out to a concert with friends and after giving me an early dinner had left me at Theo's house for a few hours.

When the news came on Mr Thorne was in the lounge downstairs watching another Star Trek episode. Theo said that his mother and father hadn't been getting along for a while and that last Christmas, to keep him out of her hair, Mrs Thorne had bought her husband every Star Trek episode and movie ever made.

Theo had examined all of the discs his mother had bought and he calculated that if you include all of the more recent versions of the show there are more than seven hundred television episodes and eleven feature films to watch. That's a lot of Star Trek footage to get through. Probably five or six hundred hours, I reckon.

I think I might have mentioned that Mr Thorne is a bit of a science fiction fan. Just as well, I suppose. Anyway, he accepted his wife's challenge with relish and no little relief and whenever he wasn't at work he could usually be found curled up in the downstairs lounge with the crew of the Starship Enterprise.

Mrs Thorne was in her bedroom getting ready to go out for a work function or dinner. These were now quite a common occurrence, according to Theo. Often she had two or three a week and on some of those occasions she didn't get home until well after midnight.

Theo, Filomena and I had been watching television in the family room upstairs. Filomena was already in her pyjamas, a pair of light blue shorts and an orange singlet. She had Tigger resting on her lap. That was very good, for me. Earlier I had fibbed to Filomena about my love of cats and now I had the perfect excuse to look in her direction frequently.

The news came on and as his sister reached for the remote to change channel Theo asked her to hold off for a moment. Filomena rolled her eyes and groaned but did as he requested.

The grey house with the green roof was on television and it was ablaze. It was furiously ablaze. The house, garage and even a few of the surrounding trees were covered in flames and thick black smoke belched into the sky. Theo and I watched in stunned silence as a part of the garage roof and wall collapsed sending up a huge shower of sparks.

The police were there in force and so was a fire crew. There were also several reporters and a number of what were presumably nosy neighbours. One of the reporters started addressing the camera. Theo and I listened, our eyes glued to the screen.

According to the reporter, armed police had raided the house yesterday in search of a senior member of a newly-formed white supremacist terrorist movement. The man was suspected of being a threat to public safety. He was wanted for questioning in relation to bomb-making materials and apparatus that had been found on the property. Those items had been purchased some time previously from a local educational supplies store.

On arriving at the dwelling and making a forced entry the police were unable to locate the wanted man. It was thought that he might have fled the day before after being tipped off by a person or persons unknown. A neighbour later reported seeing the man leave his house at high speed on a bicycle the afternoon prior to the raid.

"Well, of course he'd be going at high speed," said Theo. "The driveway down to that road is pretty flipping steep."

Having failed to locate and apprehend the suspect the police then started an extensive search of the house, finding a number of items that might be used as evidence against him. At this point an official in uniform was seen holding up a large photograph of a rough swastika on a grey background.

"What the . . .? Where did that come from?" blurted Theo.

"Beats me," I replied.

"What *are* you on about?" asked Filomena.

Theo ignored her and grabbed at my arm. "Did you see anything like that there?"

"No, of course not," I replied.

"Hang on . . . hang on a minute."

"What?"

"I reckon that's off the tail of the Messerschmitt," said Theo. "Or the Focke-Wulf. But that thing was tiny! It was nothing at all like that."

Another large printed image appeared and was held up by the official. This one depicted a German *balkenkreuz*, the black and white cross that adorned the sides of German tanks and aircraft during the war. In the image on television the cross appeared against a light blue background.

"I bet that's off the Dornier! Those things aren't that big. They're little stickers on the side of a model aeroplane. The cops have blown them up, any pinhead can see that. It's flipping obvious. This is all completely bogus!"

"What *are* you on about?" repeated Filomena.

"Quiet!" retorted Theo.

The reporter went on to say that late that afternoon, before the search of the house had been completed, a fire had started at the dwelling. It was thought to have originated from a cache of chemicals in the garage. Two policemen had narrowly escaped injury but the house was completely destroyed and any hope of finding further evidence had been lost. Other members of the terrorist movement were suspected of lighting the fire but there were no witnesses and no arrests had been made. An extensive search was now underway for the wanted man.

At this point an old photograph of Mr Richardson appeared on the screen with his name and a brief description. It looked like a driver's license, passport or work ID photo. The reporter said that this Mr Richardson had last been seen turning off Priory Road on a green bicycle with silver decals and a little flashing red light under the seat. He had been eating a banana and was wearing grey corduroy trousers, a white shirt and a yellow cardigan. Police had attempted to track the bicycle and the man's garments without success. The reporter rounded off her summary by stating that the man was thought by the police to be extremely dangerous and should not be approached by the public.

The report ended.

"So what was all that about?" asked Filomena, turning the television off. "How come you know so much about it, Theo? Was this what you were talking to Mum about yesterday?"

"Yes, it was," said Theo.

After the events of Monday afternoon and Tuesday morning Theo had felt a little bit uneasy about things and wanted to talk to someone about what we had done and why. So he sat down in the kitchen on Tuesday after school and told his mother everything. At one point Filomena had barged through the kitchen looking for a snack and her calculator and she must have picked up on something they were saying.

Mrs Thorne had listened carefully to what Theo had to say and then she told him to put it all out of his mind and forget it. Given the circumstances he had done the right thing, she said, and he had no real cause to worry. Mr Viner was a fine man, she went on, and she had known him and his family for years. He would not have sent a group of children to Mr Richardson's house if he thought there was any danger whatsoever. As a matter of fact, she went on to say, she knew something of Mr Richardson herself, from way back, and she was pretty certain that he was harmless.

Mrs Thorne carried on to say that she would call Mr Viner later that day just to make sure that everything was all right. Theo wasn't so keen on that idea, given that Mr Viner had told them not to breathe a word of their mission to anyone, but his mother told him not to worry. She would take care of Mr Viner.

Mrs Thorne then reminded Theo to always keep the 'stranger danger' mantra at the forefront of his mind and to steer clear of anyone who looked like 'a psycho, a loser or a bleeding heart liberal.'

Those were her words, not mine. I'm not entirely sure what she meant. But Mrs Thorne went on to say that she had always trusted Theo's judgement and was sure that he would be sensible about these sorts of situations in the future.

And that, as far as Mrs Thorne was concerned, was that. The matter was over and done with. She brushed aside all of Theo's questions about Mr Richardson's background, police surveillance and the persecution of the innocent with an airy laugh.

"Don't worry about any of that silly old nonsense," Mrs Thorne had said. "I'm sure that the authorities know exactly what they're doing. Would you like me to make you a milkshake?"

"But it's so unfair," complained Theo.

"I'll make you a milkshake."

"Don't you think it's unfair?"

"Chocolate or strawberry?" replied his mother.

Having already told his mother about our mischievous mission to Mr Richardson's house across the river, Theo saw no compelling reason to withhold the story from Filomena. So he told her what had happened and I added a few details where necessary.

In fact, Theo told his sister far more than he had told his mother. He told Filomena pretty well everything that I have told you, apart from the bits that would have made her angry and the bits that even he doesn't know about yet.

Theo told Filomena about the hands-free toilet paper dispenser, which she knew about already, and the full details of his work on hidden sequences and her exploding mobile phone. He told her about the pushing, shoving and name calling that was going on at school and the success of our reprisals against Wayne Galbraith and his friends using the fabulous fruit flinger. He finished up with a description of our visit in the garage from the persuasive but sinister Mr Viner and what had happened during our expedition to Mr Richardson's house.

Filomena remained quiet during all of this; she just sat there stroking Tigger and occasionally pushing a bit of her brown fringe out of her eyes. When we had finished our explanation she took a deep breath and frowned. There was silence for a moment.

"And you told all of this to Mum?" she asked. Theo shrugged and nodded.

"Well, most of it," he replied. "Okay, some of it. Mainly the bit about our visit to the house."

"And what did she say?"

"Not much, really."

Theo paused and scratched his head. Then he cast his mind back to the conversation of the previous day.

"Mum said that it was all okay; that we hadn't really done anything wrong, but that I should keep 'stranger danger' in mind in the future and not go around doing anything stupid or dangerous."

"Is that it? That's all she said? But this guy Richardson sounds like a lunatic. What did the news report say – he was making bombs or something? Mum didn't say anything about that? She didn't say anything about you going to the house of a suspected terrorist?"

"This was before the news story. And that's all garbage anyway. Mr Richardson wasn't making any bombs, he was harmless. He's no terrorist. The police just made all that stuff up."

"Why would they do that? And what caused the fire then? Why did the garage blow up?"

"The report said that someone started the fire. That doesn't mean there were chemicals in the garage."

"Did you see what was in the garage?"

"No, but . . ."

"And if Mr Richardson was so innocent, why did he take off?"

"I don't know. Maybe he was scared that the police were going to try to set him up. Which is exactly what they are doing. They're trying to set him up with all those swastikas and things."

Filomena clearly harboured some doubts about our claims of Mr Richrdson's innocence, but even she could see how lame the police assertions were with regard to the Nazi regalia. Even to her inexpert eyes the so-called 'evidence' on the television had looked ludicrous.

"I don't know about that," she said. "Well, what about all of you trespassing and breaking and entering? I mean, how stupid can you get? What did Mum have to say about that?"

"She didn't say anything about that. Later on she rang Mr Viner and he told her it was all okay. He told her to put her mind at rest and forget all about it."

Filomena shook her head in astonishment and muttered, "I can't believe it."

"It's true."

"And what about you lot ganging up on Alex Zaffino and those other kids? Did she say anything about that?"

"No, she didn't mention it. And what do you mean by that, anyway?" objected Theo. "We didn't gang up on anybody. Those bozos were ganging up on us!"

"When did they gang up on you? Those guys are useless. They couldn't gang up on anyone. They couldn't gang up on Tigger. Even Winnie would have them for breakfast."

Theo looked puzzled and scratched his head. He looked in my direction for some support or inspiration but I chose not to return his look. I kept my eyes on Filomena, who was getting quite agitated and had started bouncing around.

"Well . . . okay," said Theo. "Maybe they didn't gang up on us. But Wayne Galbraith's a pinhead and he's been calling us names. He's been really bugging us and he got Toby into a massive headlock during religious instruction. He would have torn his head clean off if the teacher hadn't stopped him."

"Yeah, right."

"It's true, I tell you."

"He would have torn his head clean off?"

"Yes."

"I don't think so."

"He would have. It was starting to go, I could see it. Another few seconds and it would have been off."

"Well, that would have made for an interesting afternoon at school."

"It's lucky for Toby the teacher stepped in when she did."

"Clearly. So the four of you decided to band together and get Galbraith back, right? And those other kids as well? Alex, Terry and Gregor? I can remember them from when I was at Hampton. Those kids are all completely harmless. They're little wimps of the highest order. Gregor Scoulidis has even got some kind of bone disease, for crying out loud."

Filomena sighed and rolled her eyes. She lifted her hand from Tigger's flank and jabbed her index finger at Theo in disgust.

"What's he ever done to you?"

Then she turned and did the same to me.

"Or you?"

I didn't like that finger jab in my direction. I don't know why but I would have preferred a massive thump or an excruciating Chinese burn. Preferably with sweat. But even though Filomena was across the room that finger jab felt almost as though she was poking me sharply in the ribs. I couldn't help but flinch.

Theo decided it was time to start fighting back. He had never liked being on the back foot where Filomena was concerned. Leaning forward on the couch he said, "Well what about Whiner – his father made us sneak in and spy on Mr Richardson. His father's a slime bucket, a thug and a liar."

"Maybe so, but just because his father is a liar and a bully that doesn't make Paul one as well. Your father can be a real loon at times too, Theo. Does that make you one?"

"Your father? What do you mean *your father*? He's not just my father. He's your father as . . ."

Filomena hadn't finished though and cut him off with a sharp wave of her hand. Theo blinked rapidly and sat back in the couch.

"Do you wanna know what I think? You know what? It's you guys who are the bullies here."

"Whaaat?" Theo was outraged.

"Yes, it's you guys. You're bullies and you're sneaks and you should be ashamed of yourselves. What on earth were you all doing breaking into Mr Richardson's house like that? Are you crazy? That is *so* against the law."

"Whiner's dad told us to."

"Viner may have told you to do it but that doesn't make it right. Adults aren't always right."

"Eh?"

"Come on, Theo, you know that most of the time they're wrong. Most of the time they talk complete rubbish. You *know* that. I shouldn't have to tell you. Look what they've done to the world. Look at the state it's in. Most of them are idiots. You should know better than to listen when some defective adult tells you to do something stupid."

We all sat in silence. Tigger yawned, stretched out a hind leg, and let out a soft meow.

I think Theo was beginning to regret telling his sister

anything at all. He was doing a bit of puffing but nothing was coming out. Finally I spoke up.

"I think that maybe Filomena's right, Theo. I think we might have gone a bit too far at school. And look what we did to Mr Richardson. We had no right to go snooping around his house. That news report is all rubbish. You know that."

"True," said Theo. "It is rubbish."

"It's all Mr Viner's doing. He probably burnt down the house, too. If it wasn't him then it was probably one of his men. Mr Richardson is none of the things that they said, they've twisted everything around. He's not dangerous at all. If anything he's one of the good guys. And now he'll probably get caught and busted and end up in jail."

Theo sat on the couch, looking at his fingers. He sighed and shook his head. Theo hated being wrong. Even more, he hated having to admit to being wrong.

"Oh, all right, you're right. You're right too, Filomena."

"Of course I am."

"I don't know what's going on. That white supremacist stuff is garbage but why did Mr Richardson have to run? What if there *were* chemicals in his garage? Mr Richardson hates all the computers, maybe he *was* planning something? Mr Viner seemed to think that he was."

"Who knows," I said. "But I think that Mr Richardson was telling us the truth. I think he just wanted to be left alone."

"Yes . . . I think so, too," agreed Theo. "You don't go planting all those vegetables and then do a runner. Those eggs needed collecting as well. Something's not right here. Something stinks."

"You can say that again," said Filomena, with a sneer. "I think it follows you around."

Theo chose to ignore that remark. He leant forward and put his head in his hands.

"This is all wrong. It's not fair. We need to do something about it. I think we need to do something about people like Mr Viner and help people like Mr Richardson. This is all crazy. We need to put it right."

"Yes, you do," said Filomena. "All of this is partly your fault. It's mainly that horrible Viner's fault, probably, but partly yours. I don't even know why you listened to Viner. He's an adult, for a start. You know as well as I do that they're all nutters. They've got no idea. But you do need to do something about all this. You need to fix it."

"Yes, but fix what exactly?" Theo, like me, was by now perplexed by the whole situation. "And how? What should we do?"

Filomena shrugged and flicked her hair off her face again. "Don't look at me, I don't know. What do you think I am? That's for you dingbats to decide."

Theo and I were stumped. It was all too much to take in. It was all too difficult. We didn't know what we should do.

We sat for a while and said nothing. Filomena stroked the cat on her lap. Theo looked at me and then looked at his sister. He looked back at me and again at his sister. Then he looked at me again but in kind of a questioning manner.

I had no idea what Theo was doing – maybe he was just feeling gassy – so I just sat there and blinked at him. Theo nodded slowly. He must have taken my blink as some kind of stamp of approval.

After a few more seconds of this I began to understand where Theo was heading with those strange expressions and head movements. Theo was secretively suggesting to me that his sister was pretty smart, in a dumb kind of way. He was saying that if she could be brought on board she might make a useful ally. Filomena had street smarts, she knew everybody and she was tougher than any kid we knew.

"Filomena," said Theo.

"Yes?"

"Will you help us?" asked Theo. "I don't know what we should do. I think we could use a little help."

Filomena pushed Tigger gently onto the floor and stood up. She walked to the window and opened it, letting in the cool evening air. Then she turned around to us.

"You want me to help you?"

"Yes."

"You're sure about that?"

"Yes."

"You can't be serious."

"We are. Really, we are."

"Gawd, you must be desperate."

"We are, we are."

"Desperate and pathetic."

"Yes, we are."

"Desperate and pathetic and stupid."

"Oh we are, we are."

"You said it."

"Hmm." Carried away by the moment, Theo wasn't sure what he'd said.

"So what do you want from me?" asked Filomena.

"I don't know. What do *you* think we should do? What do *you* suggest we do?"

"Well, I don't know. What can you do? What are your skills? You've got the science and the mechanics, Theo. That much is pretty obvious. And here you may have something of an artist. Maybe a wordsmith who's not completely crap," said Filomena, nodding at me. "But I'm not sure how useful those skills will be. This one seems to spend more time watching than doing."

"We need a good observer," said Theo.

"Yeah, right," said Filomena, sounding unconvinced.

"We've got Leroy and Toby as well," said Theo.

Filomena's face fell. Perhaps the reality of the situation, and the rather flimsy resources at our disposal, was finally dawning on her.

"Well," said Filomena, "I suppose you have. Leroy thinks he's a human weapon and Toby's busting a gut working on his ludicrous magical powers."

This reference to Toby reminded me of the episode on the school bench and I smirked to myself. Theo's sister had no idea how close she was to the truth.

"Look, we have to include Toby and Leroy, they're our friends," said Theo.

"At the moment those two are hopeless. I would say that they're more of a hindrance than a help. But yeah, I suppose they have to be part of the team. The four of you started this mess and you'll need to stick together to get out of it."

"We will stick together," Theo replied. "We're a good team. We've proven that. But will you help us, Filomena? Will you?"

Filomena frowned and looked at both of us in turn. Then she said, "You know, the two things that you lot are really missing, apart from a single brain between the four of you, are a dose of common sense and practicality. So here they are. Common sense and practicality have arrived. Courtesy of *moi*. Two for the price of one, in one fabulous package."

"So you'll help us?" asked Theo.

"Yes, Theo, I will help you."

"That's fantastic."

"I do have two conditions, though."

"Yes," said Theo. "Of course. What are they?"

"You have to stop being a knob. And your weird little friends have got to stop staring at me all the time and freaking me out."

Whoa, I thought.

Where did that come from? Did she mean Toby and Leroy?

Filomena can't have meant me, surely. I mean, she barely knew I existed. I had been watching her like a hawk for the past couple of hours and she hadn't looked at me more than twice. She can't have meant me.

It must have been Toby and Leroy. I could see why someone might think they were weird little friends. I was more like Theo's *normal* little friend.

"Okay Filomena," said Theo. "Don't worry about them. I'll make sure that they stay right away from you. And if they have to be around, I'll make sure that they don't even look at you."

Well that's brilliant, I thought. I'll bet you Theo's including me in all that.

How insulting.

"Great," said Filomena. "What a relief. Keep them away from me and this could work out well for both of us. Who knows? Maybe everything will all turn out okay."

"Maybe it will," said Theo. "Whatever *it* is."

"I'm sure you can figure out what needs to be done. Well, I'm off to bed. I'll give it some thought and we can discuss it again in the morning. I'll leave you two dipsticks to it for now."

"Okay. Good night, Filomena," said Theo.

"Good night, Filomena," I echoed, meekly.

"Good night."

"And . . . thank you, Filomena," said Theo.

"No . . . thank you, Theo," she sighed as she walked out the door.

# # # #

Further adventures of Theo, Filomena, Toby, Leroy and the rest of the gang will be available soon in *Theo Rides Again.*